HAUNTED GOLF

HAUNTED GOLF

Spirited Tales from the Rough

**Anthony Pioppi and
Chris Gonsalves**

Foreword by Peter Oosterhuis

Guilford, Connecticut

The Lyons Press is an imprint of The Globe Pequot Press.

Text design by Sheryl P. Kober

Library of Congress Cataloging-in-Publication Data is available on file.

ISBN 978-0-7627-5070-2

Printed in the United States of America

10 9 8 7 6 5 4 3 2 1

To all the teachers who took the time to foster in us our love of writing, and to all the golfers who have been and will be part of our continuing journey to embrace the wonderful game.

In memory of Randy Smith, Bob Labbance, and Hal Levy. These three, each in his own way, instilled in me a continuing desire to write and research at a level at which they would approve. —AP

In memory of my mother, Susan T. Gonsalves, who knew a great deal more about gifts than anyone I've ever met, and Howard "Hal" Peterson, the pioneer of talk radio, who also found time to teach me everything I know about playing golf. —CG

CONTENTS

CONTENTS

FOREWORD

Golf is magical and mysterious in so many ways.

People with widely differing talents for the game can play together courtesy of the handicap system. Players of all ages and both sexes can compete against one another using various teeing grounds and appropriate handicapping. Competitors with very different mind-sets can challenge each other; one can be totally focused on shot execution while the other is enjoying the walk on the beautiful links in the fresh air!

But who really knows what's lurking all around them as these players of every stripe make their way through some of the world's finest courses?

What Anthony Pioppi and Chris Gonsalves have gathered here in *Haunted Golf* is a wonderful collection of mysteries associated with this great game. We have the "Headless Frenchman"; we have Fatty Walsh's irrepressible "Gangster Ghost"; we have fascinating stories and unexplained goings-on involving legendary English golf writer Henry Longhurst. We even get to see another side to some of Greg Norman's unfortunate mishaps.

It's certainly no surprise to find that Scotland's famed St. Andrews and the Old Course are involved—that historic Musselburgh plays its part. How about Augusta National Golf Club and The Masters providing unique and unexplained circumstances? No surprise there! From South Carolina, even the oh-so-recognizable Hilton Head Island lighthouse has a story to tell.

I cannot claim any ghost stories involving my career, but I certainly feel I have been blessed with some magical experiences in this great game. After going one round with *Haunted Golf*, it's clear I need to appreciate my good luck in that regard.

Back in 1971, after two and a half years of life as a touring professional, I was picked to represent Great Britain and Ireland in the Ryder Cup matches against the United States. The match was played at Old Warson in St. Louis, Missouri. In the first-day morning foursomes of alternate-shot play, I partnered with my good friend Englishman Peter Townsend against Gardner Dickinson and the great Arnold Palmer, one of my heroes.

The first hole was a par 4. I drove and Peter found the green with our second shot, leaving the ball about forty feet from the cup. I lined up my putt, then walked to the hole to take the flagstick out. Suddenly a beautiful butterfly flew out of the hole, circled about, and then fluttered away. At first it was a shock. But the unusual event brought a smile to my lips. I returned to my ball, lined up the putt again, and proceeded to sink a forty-footer—a perfect putt clear across the green on my very first Ryder Cup hole.

What a magical moment to start my Ryder Cup career!

Equally magical was the time I won the 1981 Canadian Open at Glen Abbey outside Toronto. The great Jack Nicklaus, designer of the course and the winner of so many tournaments and championships, had a twenty-foot eagle putt at the par-5 72nd hole to tie me. I stood hanging on to the steps of the scoring trailer while Jack, unbelievably, left the putt on line but short of the cup. After several struggles and near misses, that miss by Jack gave me my first and only win on the PGA Tour. Maybe there was some unseen participant in that dramatic finish. Jack said it was a strong gust of wind that kept his ball from reaching the hole.

Ever the gracious competitor, though, Jack walked over to the trailer where I was receiving congratulations and, before going in to sign his card, stopped. He shook my hand and looked straight into my eyes.

"Congratulations, Peter," he said. "You have been very patient and now you've won one."

It was another very special spiritual moment for me!

The number thirteen may have sinister implications to some people. It has been mostly lucky for me, however. My first win as a professional came in a 1970 South African Tour event on the coast in Port Elizabeth. I shot a course-record 65 on Friday the 13th and birdied the 13th hole on the last day, holding off Gary Player in his home country and at the peak of his career.

When I was leading The Masters in 1973 after three rounds I was player number thirteen, a number assigned based on the order in which one registers. Perhaps the thirteen caused the weather problems that washed out Saturday play and had me waiting an extra day until the final round could be finished.

Not so lucky, I finished tied for third with Jack Nicklaus and Jim Jamieson. Tommy Aaron took home the green jacket.

Indeed, golf is an amazing game in so many ways, and inexplicable happenings are part of what makes it so special. I do hope you enjoy this super book.

—*Peter Oosterhuis*

INTRODUCTION

The world of golf is rife with inexplicable happenings that defy gravity and logic. Badly hit shots disappear into groves thick with trees and end up sitting quite contently on the putting green. Perfectly struck drives rocket straight and true into the blue beyond to hoots, shouts, and a chorus of "great shot!" from the playing partners and are never seen again. Any person who tees up the little white sphere has a tale that would send Sir Isaac Newton back to the apple tree and Aristotle back to Lyceum for further contemplation. It's a mysterious pursuit indeed, this game of ours.

Seasoned players learn to blame "the golf gods" and go about their rounds, trying to put the unexplained behind them. They soldier on. They take a drop, all the while knowing their ball must be nearby. They ignore sudden winds that come from nowhere on calm days to carry their shots far from their intended targets. When the ball defies all that is natural and holy to roll uphill and against the grain, they shrug and attribute it to the playful spirits that haunt most every round. Not only do golfers tolerate such madness, they embrace it. They look forward to sharing their tales and offering solace to other golfers who have experienced similarly mysterious things. Such is the game of golf.

Not every mysterious bounce or unexplained shadow can be so easily attributed to the golf gods, however. On fairways the world over, players have come face to face with experiences far more chilling. Not that they are necessarily sinister. Walk onto the world's great golf courses and you immediately sense the presence of those who came before: the Morrises, Old Tom and his son Young Tom, at the Old

Course in St. Andrew; Bobby Jones at Merion Golf Club capturing the final leg of the Grand Slam; Ben Hogan stalking Colonial Country Club's Hogan's Alley on the way to one of his five titles there. Play Pinehurst No. 2 or the National Golf Links of America and you'll "feel" the aura of architects Donald Ross and Charles Blair Macdonald—long since deceased—still watching over their prized creations.

For all its frustrations and mysteries, it's little wonder that golf is closely associated with two of the greatest horror stories ever written.

The ominous ruins of Slains Castle, reputed to be the inspiration for Bram Stoker's Dracula, loom over Cruden Bay Golf Club in northeast Scotland, though no vampires have been reported in or around the famed layout.

In *The Legend of Sleepy Hollow,* author Washington Irving described "a little valley, or rather lap of land, among the high hills, which is one of the quietest places in the whole world. A small brook glides through it, with just murmur enough to lull one to repose." That very spot is now the 3rd hole—dubbed Haunted Bridge—at Sleepy Hollow Country Club in Scarborough, New York. But if there has ever been a headless horseman or any other horrific vision on the course, Sleepy Hollow members have kept it to themselves.

In golf's long history there are, however, more than just literary creations, imagined phantoms, and weird feelings of homage to the game's pioneers. There are actual encounters with ghosts, spirits, and voices from beyond the grave.

Take, for instance, this account from a 1920 issue of *Golf Illustrated,* then one of the sport's most highly regarded magazines. According to the story, a golfer and his caddy teed off on the first hole at the famed West Links at North Berwick, Scotland. What luck this pair had! In a windswept, oceanfront region where golf has been played since the 1500s, West Links remains one of the seminal courses in golf history. It has been described as having a streak of cunning, a dash of wiliness, a touch of eccentricity, and an extra large helping of charm, all vital ingredients for true links golf.

And here this duo had the place all to themselves. There was no other soul in sight. At the second tee, however, the pair spied a mysterious player on the fairway. "The man wore clothes quite unlike those now in fashion, and there was something ceremonious about his address and subsequent stroke," the witness told the magazine. "The flight of his ball was plainly visible and it is affirmed that it started with a fair amount of pace on it but died away to nothing after having carried a hundred yards or so. Yet it seemed to have been cleanly hit with a wooden club. A feather ball might have been expected to behave in precisely this manner."

The player wondered who the man was. The caddy replied he had never seen him on the links before. When the two made their way to the second green a few minutes later, the mystery player was nowhere to be seen, leaving only one conclusion.

"Unless the eye of the spectator was deceived, the recorded facts indicate that disembodied spirits of deceased golfers can return to the scenes of their former activities," the article's author surmised.

Stories of ghosts and spirits haunting golf courses and their environs across the country and around the world continue to this day. *Haunted Golf* is a compendium of tales of the restless spirits that inhabit and grace some of golf's famous locales as well as its lesser-known tracks. Turn the pages and you'll discover the ghost of a murdered woman that continues to haunt the 7th golf hole at Victoria Golf Club in British Columbia.

Every golfer knows St. Andrews, Scotland, has a long and illustrious history as the home of golf, but few realize it also has an intensely bloody and tragic history that lasted hundreds of years. Remnants of those horrible days can still be seen in the face of the dead burned into a wall.

On the shores of New York's Otsego Lake—made famous as Glimmerglass in James Fenimore Cooper's Leatherstocking Tales—a cadre of ghosts, sometimes playful, sometimes sinister, inhabit the Otesaga Resort Hotel. Among its many attributes, the Otesaga features one of the finest resort courses in the East.

Then there's the Mount Washington Hotel in New Hampshire. Take the center staircase from the lobby to the second floor and you'll climb thirty-three stairs. Take the same route in the south wing and you'll climb just thirty-one, the intentional discrepancy designed to confuse persistent ghosts. It doesn't work. A spirit known as the Princess still keeps tabs on the guests, many of them there for the hotel's stunning eighteen-hole layout.

Spirits once inhabited the clubhouse of a San Francisco municipal course, but that's not the creepiest part of this West Coast tale. To this day, thousands of corpses remain just below the closely cropped turf in unmarked graves. The dead make their presence known with shards of bone poking through the course's manicured surface.

You'll also hear from the British golf photographer who, while covering one of the most prestigious golf tournaments in the world, learned of the death of his father while picking a flower up from the ground.

If you don't believe that the dead wander the fairways looking for their lost children or playing pranks on hotel security guards, then read on. These macabre tales of golf and ghosts will surely quicken your pulse and change your mind. Then, when you take to the links and witness the mysterious, the bizarre, the inexplicable—and you surely will—you'll forever wonder whether it's merely the golf gods, or perhaps something far more sinister at work.

Chapter 1

Victoria Golf Club: Murder on the 7th Fairway

Victoria Golf Club has one of the most scenic stretches of seaside holes in all of Canadian golf; it also has one of the country's most macabre tales of murder-suicide. Although the killer has been long forgotten, the victim continues to haunt the course's visitors— especially young lovers—who dare wander near the place where she met her violent end.

Doris Gravlin saw her patient off to sleep, then settled in for a quiet night in the apartment where she lived and worked as a private nurse. It was unusually mild on the evening of September 22, 1936. Doris watched the resulting fog roll in from the Strait of Juan de Fuca and envelop the little town of Oak Bay at the southern tip of Canada's Vancouver Island. With the steady thrum of the Pacific Ocean as a backdrop, the young nurse retired to her room and reflected on how far short her life had fallen from her young-girl dreams.

Some twenty-two years before that night, she had been Doris Thompson, a gregarious eight-year-old enchanted by her new home in the bustling seaport of nearby Victoria, British Columbia. Her family had just arrived from Lancashire, England, part of a growing wave of immigrants flocking to the area looking for work as loggers or fishermen or in one of the many paint factories that dotted the region. The weather in Victoria is among the mildest in all of Canada, and Doris was immediately enchanted with Victoria's lush gardens, picturesque lanes, and the towering stone buildings and luxury hotels of the prosperous provincial capital. When her mother, Charlotte, found work as a nurse in Victoria's Sunhill Sanitarium, Doris decided that she too wanted to work in medicine, helping to care for the wealthy and powerful drawn to Victoria's combination of metropolitan and resort amenities.

Yes, she had indeed become a nurse. Yet, now here she was, a thirty-year-old woman alone in her room, her marriage in tatters and her young son living with his grandmother while she tended to the day-to-day needs of Kathleen Richards, an elderly resident of Oak Bay's tony waterfront. Her one remaining pleasure was taking afternoon strolls through the nearby Victoria Golf Club. She loved the contrast of the manicured golf course set against the raw, natural beauty of the western Canadian coast. She was drawn to the place. If only her life could be that neat and beautiful, she thought.

She felt herself about to cry but was startled back to reality by insistent rapping at the door. She peered through the curtains and saw a boy clutching an envelope. It was the nephew of her estranged husband, Victor Gravlin. She opened the door.

"What are you doing about at this hour?" she asked the lad.

"Uncle Victor sent me with this," he replied, thrusting the note in her direction. "He told me to give you this."

"Was he drunk? Of course he was, what am I saying? He's always drunk. Anyway, tell him I don't want it. I don't want to hear a thing from him."

"Please, Auntie Doris. He'll only make me come back here. Please take it. I don't like to be out here when it's dark and foggy like this. I'm scared and I want to go home."

His voice trailed off and it broke her heart. He looked so small with the thick salt mist swirling around him.

"You don't even have to read it," the boy muttered.

"Give it to me," Doris said to the boy. She took the envelope and removed its contents, a single sheet of paper, a handwritten note from Victor. By the dim light leaking out onto the porch, Doris Gravlin read the note and her face went slack and pale.

"Tell him I'll be there," she said without looking up. "Go. Run and tell him."

Not needing to hear it a second time, the boy ran off.

Back inside, Doris pulled on her pink sweater and grabbed her hat. Before heading out, she checked in on Mrs. Richards, who stirred only slightly when Doris whispered that she was going out to talk with Victor.

"Take care out there, Doris," the old woman told her.

"Yes, missus. I shan't be gone long."

As she walked toward Beach Road, Doris pulled her hat down tighter against the thickening fog. Going to see Victor at this hour mostly frightened and annoyed her. There was a time not long ago, however, when rushing to see Victor would have thrilled her into breathlessness. When they had met through a mutual acquaintance in 1928, he was a dashing athlete—seven years her senior—from a family of athletes. All of the Gravlin boys were well-known native sons in Victoria. Victor's brother, Walter, played professional baseball in the Northwest League, based in the United States, before becoming head professional at Uplands Golf Club in Victoria.

Victor himself was a sports writer for the local paper, the *Colonist,* as well as an avid fisherman and accomplished golfer. It was Victor who had introduced Doris to the stunning beauty of the Victoria Golf Club. They'd strolled the coastline that bordered the course's 2nd through 10th holes countless times during their courtship. Victor regaled his young fiancée with tales about the place. He told her how local amateur player Harry Comb laid out Victoria Golf Club's first nine holes in 1893, making it the second oldest course in Canada and one of the oldest in North America. Doris took it all in with the rapt attention of a young woman deeply in love.

And so it was to Victoria Golf Club that Doris was headed on the night of September 22, 1936, to meet her estranged husband. The note his nephew had delivered earlier that evening was never found, so it remains unclear what Victor wrote to convince Doris to meet with him on that dreary autumn night. But as everyone in town knew, Victor's plunge into alcoholism, the vice that wrecked the couple's six-year marriage, hadn't dampened his desire to reunite with his wife and son. He continued to muddle through his days in the *Colonist*'s sports department and spent his nights in his parents' house in a growing, drunken depression. That night, shortly after he'd dispatched his nephew, Victor told his mother and father that he was stepping out for a while.

Several people reported seeing Victor and Doris walking together on Beach Road near the Victoria Golf Club later that night. It was the last time either would be seen alive. Intimately familiar with the course layout, an inebriated Victor lured Doris to a secluded grove of trees that separated the 6th green and 7th tee. At first, he tried to win her back near the place where they'd first professed their love.

"Please," Victor slurred. "Our son needs his father. I want us together, all of us, as a family. We should be in our own home again. Don't you want that as well?"

The smell of whiskey and sweat turned her stomach. She couldn't muster the words to rebuff him. She'd loved him once, but now he was broken and pitiful. How could she tell him that a home and a family were what she wanted more than anything. Just not with him. Not with what he had become.

"Coming here was a mistake," she said. "I'm sorry, Victor. I'm leaving."

"Doris," he begged, "I have nothing left. Nothing. Do you understand? I cannot bear this any longer. We must be together."

Doris turned toward the ocean and breathed deep of the salt air. Even in darkness the place had a raw, powerful presence. If only life could be this neat and beautiful, she thought. She took it all in one last time. Without warning, Victor whipped a narrow cord around her throat and pulled it taut.

"We'll be together this night," Victor snarled as he tightened the rope with all of his strength. Doris fell to her knees, then thrashed weakly as she slipped from consciousness and into death. The mother of his child dead at his feet, Victor Gravlin set about trying to conceal his foul deed. He dragged Doris's body down the 7th fairway to a notch in the craggy shoreline and covered her as best he could with stones and twigs. In a final indignity, he rolled a large log over Doris's corpse and ran from the scene.

Later that night, Mrs. Richards awoke and called for Doris. The old woman vaguely recalled the young nurse saying she was stepping out to meet her estranged husband, but clearly she should be back home by now. When she got no response, Mrs. Richards called the police, who immediately began searching for Doris. Investigators called Victor's parents, who told them their son had gone out earlier in the evening and hadn't returned either. Police combed the area for days but found no trace of the troubled couple. Most townspeople feared the worst, and with four days gone and no sign of Victor or Doris, many felt the mystery might never be solved.

Less than a week later, however, a young Victoria Golf Club caddy looking for errant golf balls on the rock-strewn shoreline saw a bit of pink fabric peeking from beneath a log to the left of the 7th green. When the boy tried to retrieve the item, he discovered to his horror that it was a sweater—still wrapped about the crushed, lifeless body of Doris Gravlin. Police determined that Doris had been strangled elsewhere on the course and dragged to the spot where the log had been shoved on top of her. What perplexed them most about the crime, though, was that her shoes and her hat were missing. They would not have to wait long for the mystery to be solved.

Within a week, a local fisherman rowing his way through beds of kelp—long, tubular seaweed that grows in thick clumps—came across the body of a man floating in the tangle of dark green. The fisherman left the body there and returned to shore, where he summoned the authorities. Authorities brought the decaying corpse to land, where it was identified as Victor Gravlin. In his pockets were the hat and shoes of his dead wife, as well as an eighteen-inch piece of rope police said he had used to strangle Doris. Detectives surmised that after choking the life out of Doris and rolling the log on top of her, a guilt-ridden Victor simply walked into the ocean to take his own life. Victor's mother, however, refused to believe the official version and, until the day she died, claimed that her son was an innocent murder victim and the target of a frame-up. Residents in the Victoria area discounted her accusations and ostracized Victor's family. After Doris's murder, folks in the area would get up and change seats if a Gravlin sat next to them on a trolley.

Doris and Victor were soon buried and their young son returned with Doris's grief-stricken family to England. But Doris was clearly not content to be with Victor in this life or the afterlife, and she most certainly would not let her murder be forgotten. Within a few months of the slaying, word began to swirl around Victoria of a ghost in the shape of a woman haunting the area of Victoria Golf Club's 7th green, near where Doris's body had been found. The clearly agitated spirit of Doris Gravlin appears to some as a glowing ball of light hovering near the 7th hole. To others, she shows up as a woman in white, a wedding dress perhaps, gliding down the 7th fairway before vanishing suddenly. Doris's heartbreak and failed marriage play a key role in the hauntings, the locals insist. Young lovers unfortunate enough to witness the apparition of Doris Gravlin will never marry, the legend has it.

Although Victor Gravlin's ghost has never been seen—proof, some say, that he really did commit murder—Doris's ghost continues to haunt Victoria Golf Club with increasing frequency with each passing year. Especially during April and on nights with a full moon, the restless spirit of Doris Gravlin menaces nighttime visitors to the popular oceanfront course. When a local newspaper, the *Daily Columnist,* ran a story about encounters with Doris's ghost in the mid-1960s, area residents flooded the paper with their own reports of strange happenings near the club's 7th hole. Over time, they said, Doris's ghost has become more "defined" and aggressive.

No story better illustrates that than a recent tale that begins with a simple family fishing trip. A few years ago, an elderly couple brought their two young grandchildren to the rocky shore near Victoria Golf Club's 7th green for some fishing. In short order, the grandson hooked something. Unfortunately, it was the side of his grandmother's head, which he'd snagged while trying to make a cast. The four went off to the hospital so Grandma could have the hook removed. As if the grandson didn't feel bad enough already, while at the hospital he realized his grandfather had left their tackle box back on the shoreline.

It was night when the four returned to Beach Drive. The grandfather and grandson went back to the fishing spot while the grandmother and granddaughter remained in the car. The boy and his grandfather got the tackle box and were on the way back to the car when they encountered the ghost of Doris. She was in an especially aggressive mood on this particular evening. The murdered woman's spirit came running at the grandfather and the boy in the form of a screaming apparition dressed in flowing white, her face frozen in a twisted combination of fear and rage. The ghost flew up and over the terrified pair and continued out and over the family's car. The frightened grandfather and the boy raced back to the vehicle, where the two women were cringing and screaming in horror.

In another instance, Doris took on a quieter, more amorphous but no less disturbing form. A couple walking the club's 7th fairway at night saw a large globe of light rushing toward them. The light flew silently up and over them and then descended on their car, engulfing it. They debated running in the opposite direction but at last decided the car, however surrounded by the mysterious force, remained their best bet. The couple jumped in their illuminated vehicle and sped off, leaving the eerie, unexplained light in the spot where they had been parked.

Doris's ghost has changed her methods many times in the ensuing decades, witnesses say. For instance, very near the spot where Doris was actually killed behind the 6th green there hangs a bell normally rung by golfers heading to the 7th tee to let players on the fairway know the green—which golfers on the fairway cannot see—is clear. Ringing the bell at night is now considered a surefire way to summon Doris's spirit. "Every high school student heads down to the course and rings the bell," says former Canadian government historian John Adams, now an authority on hauntings in greater Victoria. Adams, who has spent more than twenty-five years documenting sightings of Doris Gravlin's ghost, says he is not surprised by how many people have had experiences in and around Victoria Golf Club. He leads a bus tour of haunted locales in and around Victoria with stops along Beach Drive, where riders get out to see the 7th fairway while Adams recounts the tale.

"When I ask if anyone is familiar with the ghost, we always get people who come forward and say, 'Yes, yes, I've seen it,'" he says.

The Victoria Golf Club clubhouse is also the scene of some mysterious happenings, though nobody is sure whether they're related to Doris. On many occasions, night security personnel say, they've heard music and footsteps in empty buildings. And one night watchman in particular claims on several occasions to have left an empty clubhouse to make his nightly rounds only to find a single rose placed on his desk when he returned. He never found out why he was receiving the gift or who was leaving the memento behind. Perhaps Doris couldn't help but show her appreciation for one man near her making good on his promises and responsibilities.

Or perhaps Victoria Golf Club has other ghosts, spirits less bitter and disenchanted with romance than Doris Gravlin.

Chapter 2

Trails West Golf Course: Catherine Sutler's Eternal Search

Fort Leavenworth is the oldest active U.S. Army base west of the Mississippi. Tens of thousands of soldiers have passed through the base, from Dwight D. Eisenhower to George Custer. No one, though, has left a legacy as frightening as that of Catherine Sutler, who has been haunting the base's golf course since it opened.

"Ethan! Mary! Stay where I can see you now. And mind the hour. We'll be leaving soon."

Tears welled in Catherine Sutler's eyes as she watched for the very last time her young son and daughter run barefoot through the ryegrass that surrounded their small farm in southwestern Indiana. She paused while locking the farmhouse door, her finger tracing the notches in the molding that marked the heights of her quickly growing children. Had Ethan ever been that small? She wondered. Was Mary already seven years old?

Lost in her reverie, she was startled when Hiram snuck up behind her and grabbed her by the waist. "Don't tell me my wife is getting nostalgic for this old place," Hiram chided her. "We're on to a life much bigger and better than this,

Catherine. Finish saying goodbye to the old house, then gather the children and let's be on our way."

"Are you sure about this, Hiram?" Catherine asked.

"As sure as I love you," Hiram said, with a peck on her cheek. "Come on, now. The new owners will be here soon, and they won't want the likes of us about. Leave the key by the windowsill and let's go. Westward, ho!"

Hiram cut such a vibrant, strapping figure, how could she doubt him? It was early fall of 1880. The weather was still hot, and she watched him sweat and strain as he busied himself securing the last of their belongings onto the wagon. She began to take heart. Their family farm had been sold. They were about to join tens of thousands of other young Americans who'd already set out to take advantage of the recently opened Oregon territory, an area that included what today covers Washington, Oregon, Idaho, and parts of Wyoming and Montana. Hiram had told her each married couple that made the arduous journey west was entitled to 640 acres of free land. For the sake of her family—for the future of the children she loved more than life itself—she was willing to give up everything she held dear.

"Ethan! Mary! Come now. We're leaving."

She gathered her children to her side, pulling them close, holding them one last time in front of the weathered, familiar farm. "You two stay close to your mother, you hear?" she said without scolding. "No matter what, I'll always protect you."

The journey across southern Illinois was hard but uneventful; Catherine and her young family made the best of the conditions by inventing games with whatever was at hand. Ethan and Mary spent hours playing "graces," tossing a hoop cut from a tin of beans between two sticks. At night, the family sat shoulder to shoulder while Catherine prayed for their safety and success. Then the Sutlers went to sleep in the shadow of the wagon that held everything they owned in the world.

Several weeks into their arduous travels, the Sutlers made camp near Platte City, Missouri.

"It's time we had a break and got our provisions in order. I have a cousin stationed on the Army base across the river, there," Hiram said, pointing toward the west. "We can stop there and rest awhile before moving on. It will be good for the kids."

As anxious as Catherine was to put the cross-country adventure behind her, the thought of spending some time in the safety and relative comfort of a military post thrilled her. Perhaps the children would have a chance to play and swim and stretch their young legs. The trip had been hardest on them so far, she thought.

Catherine Sutler stood on the eastern bank of the Missouri River looking at the darkening mass where Fort Leavenworth rose from the rolling Kansas countryside. "I think that will be just fine," she said to Hiram. But almost as soon as the words left her lips, an icy blast rolled up off of the muddy river, cooling the warm autumn night and chilling her to the bone. She stood frozen in fear for several minutes until the feeling passed. "I'm just exhausted," she told herself. She made dinner and went to sleep early with Ethan and Mary on either side of her. Tomorrow was a big day, she thought.

After nearly a month of traveling the open prairie, Catherine was amazed by Fort Leavenworth's magnificent stone buildings. Workers were putting the finishing touches on a school for officers that would become known as the

Command and General Staff College. Chain gangs of prisoners were completing no less impressive a facade on a building simply marked "U.S.D.B." Despite the cryptic moniker, the nature of the workforce and the bars installed on all the windows made it clear to Catherine. This was a prison. The U.S. Disciplinary Barracks, or "the castle," would become the military's only maximum-security jail and the only one with a death row. Only enlisted soldiers with sentences of more than seven years, commissioned officers, and prisoners convicted of national security–related offenses would be sent to Leavenworth's harsh "castle."

The remainder of the fort was a patchwork of crisp, green parade fields, rolling grass hills, ponds teeming with catfish and a serenity she hadn't seen since she'd left Indiana. With Ethan and Mary in tow, she walked the placid meadows along Merritt Lake and around the cemetery near the center of the military reservation. Whenever she ventured near the Missouri River, which marked Leavenworth's eastern border, however, she felt the same gripping chill that had stopped her in her tracks in Platte City.

"That's just old George Armstrong Custer," Hiram's cousin told her when she mentioned her unsettling experience. "He's been haunting the place these past five years, you know. He may have died a general at the hands of the Sioux, but his spirit never got over being busted to lieutenant colonel right here at Leavenworth thirteen years ago. He lost a year's pay for running off from his unit to visit his wife.

"I'll bet those 260 men in the 7th Cavalry who died with him at Little Bighorn wish he'd never been put back in command, eh? But I guess Ol' George had seen enough of Indian territory in this life. His ghost decided to make Leavenworth its stomping grounds. Folks see him all the time, especially up by the commander's house," he said.

Catherine shuffled uncomfortably.

"And that's not all," the young soldier went on. "There's homes here on this post with more ghosts than people in them. See that place over there?" He pointed to a dark mansard roof two blocks over on Sumner Place.

"That's the oldest house on Fort Leavenworth and the most haunted house in all of Kansas," he told Catherine. "I heard a woman was murdered there. If you sit quietly in that house on a moonless night, she'll appear at the end of the hall, then charge at you, shrieking and trying to claw at you with her fingernails. And if it's not her, it'll be the spirit of an old woman who just sits in the shadows in a rocking chair talking to herself, or the ghost of a boy who throws violent temper tantrums, then disappears in a flash.

"It's quite a collection of spooks we have here, I tell ya."

"Please stop," pleaded Catherine, pulling her dark shawl tighter against the crisp fall air. "I don't need to hear all of this."

"I'm sorry," the soldier said. "I just thought you'd want to know that it wasn't just you. That you weren't, you know, going crazy. Why, right there on Sumner there's a place where the ghost of the old housekeeper floats around in her black woolen shawl, still washing dishes and making beds and calming fussy children.

"They tried to perform an exorcism to get her out," he said, "but the ghost just moved next door. So they exorcised that house and the ghost moved right back. Seems to me that just about anyone who dies around Fort Leavenworth is likely to haunt the place in some form or another."

Catherine didn't like all this talk of ghosts and death. The next day she started pressuring Hiram to move on from the post and resume their trip westward.

"A few more days," Hiram told her. "Keep the faith, my dear. We'll be on our way directly."

Early one evening, with a slight fall chill coming on, Hiram sent the children to find some more wood for the family's campfire. "Go down by the river, where the driftwood has washed up high on the banks," he told them. "Bring back as much as you can carry."

Ethan and Mary tore off in pursuit of the wood but were stopped short by the shouts of their mother. "And be careful, you two! Don't go near the water! And be back before it gets dark, you hear?"

"Yes, ma'am," they answered in unison. And off they ran. It was the last time Catherine Sutler would ever see her precious children.

Ethan and Mary raced down along the river, glad for the chance to be out from under their mother's watchful eye and thrilled to be helping out in the grand frontier adventure their family's life had become. The children played a game of one-upmanship, each trying to gather the largest bundle of bleached and sun-dried driftwood. They raced carefree down the Missouri's slick, silty bank. Ethan was stooping to add another log to his load when he heard his sister's screams. By the time he looked up she was already bobbing just above the surface of the muddy water and moving downstream impossibly fast.

"Help me," Mary managed weakly before the river spun her around and away from Ethan, taking her.

Instinctively Ethan ran into the river and found himself in the grip of the inky water. He slid forward on the slick stones, falling to his knees. He tried crawling forward but the river grabbed him and spun him around, dunking him under, then spitting him back up to the surface. His hands and feet flailed but found no purchase. Barely managing to keep his head above the water, he was helpless. He looked back at the shore and saw the pile of wood he'd collected shrinking in the distance. Would his father ever find it? he wondered. Would they ever find him and Mary? Was he about to die? The walls of Fort Leavenworth disappeared in the dark as the cold water carried the boy downstream, chilling him into paralysis.

"Mama!" he cried. The rushing water stole his voice. The boy struggled to breathe. From somewhere behind him he heard his sister cry out.

"Mama, help!"

At that very instant, at the opposite end of Fort Leavenworth, Catherine felt as though her heart had frozen in her chest. She let out a tortured gasp, then ran to her husband.

"Hiram! The children! They've been gone more than an hour. Please go check on them."

"Oh, Catherine, they're fine. Probably gathered more wood than they can carry," Hiram said. But when he saw the look of terror on his young wife's face, he relented. "I'll go find them, give them a hand with their loads."

Catherine watched her husband walk east toward the river, telling herself she was foolish to be so worried about them. Soon they would come back with enough wood for a week and they'd all sleep warm and close and safe. But when she saw Hiram running back toward the campsite, panicked and sweating, she dropped to her knees and sobbed loudly. She didn't need to hear the words. Hiram said them anyway.

"The children! I've looked everywhere! They're gone, Catherine. It's like they just vanished!"

Hiram ran to gather a group to help search for his children, but Catherine was frozen in her anguish. While the rest of the search party concentrated on the riverbank where the children were last seen, the young mother wrapped in her black shawl took a carriage lantern and wandered aimlessly toward the parklike woodland at the center of the fort. She moved across Leavenworth's rolling hills and between the tombstones of the post's nearby sprawling cemetery, calling forlornly, "Ethan? Mary? Ethan? Mary? Are you there?"

Hiram was joined by soldiers from the base and residents of the town, many carrying torches to light their way. The search was called off when it became too dark to continue, but at first light the next day, the hunt resumed with even more soldiers and civilians joining the search party. Catherine watched helplessly as boats were dispatched to search the opposite bank of the Missouri River and to drag the muddy water. She could read the disappointment in the faces of the men as they returned with nothing to show for their efforts. After a week of fruitless searching, the recovery effort was called off and Hiram and Catherine were left alone to absorb the brutal reality that their children were lost and presumed dead.

"We can't continue on, Catherine," Hiram told his wife. "There's nothing out west for us now. Let's go back to Indiana. We can buy back the farm. We can go back home. What's left of our lives is there."

But Catherine would not be lured away from Leavenworth so easily. While Hiram worked to make arrangements for a return trip east, Catherine spent each day and night wandering the fields and forests of the Army post, lantern in hand, searching for her lost children. "Ethan? Mary?" her only words. Deep into the frigid winter of 1880, Catherine, wearing only her housedress and dark shawl and carrying her lantern, continued to comb Leavenworth's grounds calling for her missing son and daughter. Finally her sadness, coupled with exposure to the harsh Kansas winter, took its toll. A brokenhearted Catherine Sutler died of pneumonia in early spring 1881, the names of her children the last words on her lips.

Hiram Sutler returned to Indiana, having apparently lost his entire young family in his quest to realize the frontier dream. And so he believed, until several weeks later when the unthinkable happened.

Back at Fort Leavenworth, spring had begun in earnest. In addition to the greening of the hills and the blooming of the vast fields of sunflowers in eastern Kansas, the warmer weather signaled the return of a band of Meskwaki Fox Indians. This particular tribe of Fox were well known for summering in the Dakotas, then moving down through Kansas and Missouri to winter in Oklahoma. When they returned to the Leavenworth area in the spring of 1881, an English-speaking member of the tribe contacted Army authorities.

"At the end of the last harvest, we had traveled fully two days south of your Army camp when we heard a great screaming," the Indian emissary told Leavenworth officers. "A boy and a girl were being swallowed by the river. Two braves jumped in to save them or they would have surely died.

"Since our tribe was already moving south, we had no choice but to bring the children along for the winter and care for them as if they were our own," the Indian said. "We knew we would return here in the spring and bring them back. See how fit and strong they are, and how well we have cared for them."

With that, the Fox tribesman turned over to the stunned Army officials a perfectly healthy Ethan and Mary Sutler.

When word reached Hiram Sutler in Indiana, he was overjoyed. He quickly made arrangements to travel back to Kansas. What remained of the Sutler family was reunited at Fort Leavenworth in the spring of 1881. Ethan and Mary mourned the loss of their mother. Then, father, son, and daughter journeyed back to Indiana, finishing what should have been the final chapter in the Sutler family's ill-fated attempt at pioneering.

But almost as soon as the living Sutlers had left Leavenworth for good, Catherine Sutler reappeared.

For several years, soldiers stationed at Fort Leavenworth reported seeing the ghost of Catherine wandering through the night in the same dark outfit she wore while alive, lantern in hand, calling for her children. The sightings at first were limited to the base graveyard, but in 1920, a large swath of the hilly meadows and woodland abutting the cemetery was turned into Leavenworth's Trails West golf course. The 6,188-yard, par-71 course gave countless officers attending the fort's famed Command and General Staff College—alumni include military greats George S. Patton, Douglas MacArthur, Dwight D. Eisenhower, and Colin Powell—a chance to play golf while studying at the advanced warfare school.

Trails West also gave the ghost of Catherine Sutler her preferred haunt. Unaware that her children survived their encounter with the Missouri River and lived to ripe old ages back in Indiana, Catherine continues to this day to search for them. Countless visitors to Trails West say they've seen her shawl-draped specter moving along the course fairways, her lantern flickering behind the hedgerows, as she calls out in vain for Ethan and Mary.

Of course, Catherine Sutler isn't the only spirit haunting the nation's oldest Army base west of the Mississippi. In the years since Catherine's death, Fort Leavenworth has gained infamy as the military's largest prison, a place where many U.S. and enemy soldiers met their deaths at the end of a rope. And in addition to the neat rows of white stones—grave markers for America's honored veterans—at Leavenworth's national cemetery, the post is also home to the Military Prison Cemetery, where deceased prisoners whose family members never claimed their bodies are interred.

During World War II, Nazi prisoners of war were housed at the fort prison, and fourteen were executed for crimes committed against other POWs, including Allied informants. All were hanged during a two-day period in 1945, the last mass execution conducted by the U.S. military. The ghosts of the German soldiers, who according to legend were hanged in an elevator shaft, still haunt Leavenworth's building 65. Guards have reported hearing the shrill screams of the executed soldiers coming from the shaft.

In 1961 Army Private John Bennet became the last person executed in the prison and the last execution by the U.S. military. He was hanged for the rape and attempted murder of an eleven-year-old Austrian girl, even though the victim and her parents asked that his life be spared. On the day of his execution, Bennet sent a telegram to President John F. Kennedy asking that his sentence be commuted. He never received a response.

But for all of the other violence, mayhem, death, and supernatural activity in and around Leavenworth, it's the quiet, forlorn spirit of Catherine Sutler that still haunts the

old Army post and its golf course most frequently. Perhaps it's the heartbreaking nature of her death, or the tragic misunderstanding that fueled her great sadness. For whatever reason, on crisp fall nights when dusk descends over the hills and swales of the Trails West course, there's always a chance to see a brief lantern flicker and witness Catherine's ghost continuing her endless search for the children she never found.

Listen close and you'll hear Catherine's plaintive cry: "Ethan? Mary? Are you there?"

Chapter 3

Mount Washington Hotel and Resort: The Princess Still Reigns

The Mount Washington Resort Hotel is a jewel of New Hampshire's White Mountains with a restored Donald Ross track so scenic and delicious, slugger Babe Ruth kept a locker at the clubhouse. But those who see the place for the first time don't think golf; they immediately, if mistakenly, connect it with writer Stephen King's The Shining. In fact, the hotel's most frequent ghost, the Princess, could easily be a character in a King novel—except that she's real.

The young bride sat staring at her husband's casket. She was numb. How could such a seemingly charmed life have turned so sour so quickly?

Just a year before, Carolyn Foster Stickney, the beautiful daughter of a Boston butcher, had stood at her husband's side on a sparkling summer day at what seemed like the top of the world. In the shadow of New Hampshire's Mount Washington, the couple presided over the grand opening of the most magnificent hotel Carolyn had ever seen. It was 1902 and the Mount Washington Resort was already being hailed as the crown jewel of New York coal baron and developer Charles Stickney's collection of luxury hotels.

As her husband had chatted with the dignitaries assembled for the event, Carolyn had shielded her eyes against the blazing July sunshine and watched as some of the 350 staff members in crisp white uniforms began the task of bringing the grand new hotel to life. Workers and guests alike moved in and out of the main entrance oohing and aahing at the Mount Washington's twenty-three-foot-high ceilings, its Turkish baths, its billiard room and bowling alley.

Carolyn had wandered over to the magnificent veranda that wrapped around the back of the hotel and perched herself on one of the wicker chairs that faced the towering vista of Mount Washington, the highest peak in the northeastern United States. From here she'd seen folks milling about the nine-hole golf course across the road, part of the Mount Pleasant House, which her husband had also built. The Mount Pleasant was a beautiful place in its own right, but today all eyes were on the new Mount Washington Hotel. The golfers pointed and waved.

"You must be very proud," the wife of one of the VIPs had whispered to her. How could she even begin to explain?

She was Carolyn Foster from the blue-collar town of Waltham, Massachusetts. Her father owned a meat stall in Boston's Faneuil Hall that included among its clients many of the hotels of the White Mountains. In the early 1890s, Carolyn had met Joseph at another New Hampshire resort, the Twin Mountain House, where her family and his spent part of their summer vacations. Not that Carolyn's family ran in the same circles as Joseph's. When summer ended for him, it was off to Paris or to one of his mansions in Westchester County, New York. For her it was back to Waltham.

She hadn't thought much of Joseph during their chance first encounter. Yes, he was rich and charming, but he was also almost thirty years older than her. She'd seen him watching her and she thought perhaps he was interested when he came around occasionally to make small talk, but she had passed it off as an innocent summer flirtation. Later that year, when Joseph had sailed his yacht, the *Susquehanna,* with its crew of twenty-five, into Boston Harbor, she heard about it but had no real expectations. Then a friend of a friend invited her aboard Joseph's magnificent boat for an evening dinner cruise. Her heart leapt a little and she quickly accepted. She was surprised at her own excitement over the chance to see Joseph again.

She knew now that she'd walked straight into his heart that night aboard the *Susquehanna.* She may have been poor and she may have been young, but she'd never once doubted that Joseph had fallen deeply in love with her right then. He'd pursued her relentlessly until the day they were married in 1892.

And now here she was, a widow at thirty-four years of age. Joseph had died suddenly of natural causes at the age of sixty-two. Rich and powerful people, many of the same folks who had helped celebrate the Mount Washington's unveiling, were now assembled to eulogize her dead husband. But she barely heard what they were saying. She pulled her coat up tighter against the chill December wind and watched J. Pierpont Morgan and William Rockefeller don gloves to help carry her husband's casket to his grave.

She'd need the help of these savvy, successful businessmen, she thought. Through her sadness it began to dawn on her that she was now alone and in charge of the Mount Washington Hotel.

"I'm so sorry for your loss, Carolyn," a VIP's wife had said to her.

The hotel that the widowed Carolyn Foster Stickney returned to manage by herself in December 1903 looked, at least outwardly, very much as it does today. Though offering its guests every creature comfort in a stunning natural setting amid the White Mountains' Presidential Range, it is still an imposing, intimidating sight. For many visitors, the first glimpse of the grand hotel in Bretton Woods, New Hampshire, conjures up images of Stanley Kubrick's horror film *The Shining*. The movie stars Jack Nicholson, Shelley Duvall, and Danny Lloyd as the only winter residents of the fictional Overlook Hotel, which, unbeknownst to them, possesses an inherent evil that eventually drives Nicholson's character to insanity and murder.

While Mount Washington, with its stark Spanish Renaissance Revival architecture set against a snow-capped mountain backdrop, does bear some resemblance to the setting used for the 1980 movie (it's actually the Timberline Lodge at the base of Oregon's Mount Hood) it was not even the inspiration for the Stephen King novel on which the film is based. In fact, King, a native of neighboring Maine, claims he'd never been to the place before writing *The Shining*.

Although the hotel may not have inspired the well-known tale of terror, there is still an undeniable common denominator between the fictitious Overlook and the real Mount Washington Resort. As Scatman Crothers's character, Dick Hallorann, says in *The Shining*, "Some places are like people: Some shine and some don't."

In fact, it seems the architect, Charles Alling Gifford, and the 250 Italian craftsmen brought to New Hampshire to build the resort may have had an inkling that the place would one day be the realm of guests both living and dead. The Mount Washington is constructed such that guests heading to the second floor from the lobby must climb thirty-three stairs. Those going up from the South Tower, though, climb only thirty-one steps. Could it be an effort to confuse the ghosts? According to the history of the hotel, the difference in the stairs was done precisely to fool the ghosts. Or is it merely superstition that came along with the European artisans who built the hotel? Perhaps the builders knew that one day one of their own employers would be wandering the hotel's halls, haunting her former suite as an apparition.

The hotel itself may have been giving off an unusual energy, a supernatural vibe. But by early 1904, one thing decidedly not shining was Carolyn's outlook on life. Once so full of vigor, Carolyn had been the first woman to swim in the Mount Washington Resort's outdoor pool. Now, despite still being young, rich, and beautiful, she became a virtual recluse in the hotel. She was a sort of living ghost in the place, moving in and out of the shadows in her own little world of silence and sadness.

It wounded the staff to see their kindhearted boss so crushed and inconsolable. Employees would often see the heartbroken Carolyn peering down through the thin curtains covering her balcony as guests descended the main staircase on their way to dinner. Once they were all seated, only then would she slip into her private dining room and eat alone in silence.

Despite her malaise, she did manage several important improvements at the Mount Washington, including her part in the commissioning of master designer Donald Ross to develop an eighteen-hole golf course at the resort. The course replaced the nine-hole track her husband had developed at Mount Pleasant, the work of Scottish designer Alex Findlay. The eighteen-holer would become one of the resort's feature attractions over the next century. The course Ross designed in 1913, however, remains almost as mysterious as the grand old hotel it surrounds.

Ross provided detailed plans for every hole, showing specific locations and dimensions for bunkers and mounds, not something he did for every job, which led to the conclusion he was paid handsomely for the work. The investment was worthwhile, as one of the preeminent architects of the day turned in a stellar effort. What Ross drew up was a stunning golf course that rivaled the best he had come up with to that point in his illustrious career. For unknown reasons, however, the course was never built to his plans. Maybe it was an economic decision or perhaps some believed that the design was too difficult for hotel guests who were looking for a leisurely round of golf. What was eventually built in 1915 had hints of Ross's work but in no way had his intended flair or drama.

With the work of Ross and other hotel contractors largely in the hands of underlings, Carolyn began spending more and more time in France. But nearly a decade after her husband passed away, she was still deeply blue. She adopted a life of quiet, rather dismal solitude. The widow was still worth more than $10 million, but to Carolyn, happiness seemed priceless.

In 1912, Carolyn Foster Stickney's life took a dramatic turn for the better. At the age of forty-three, she met Prince Aymon de Faucigny-Lucinge of Paris. Newspaper accounts of the day say that from the moment they met, he "pursued his suit for her hand with ardor." After a whirlwind romance, the two were married in London in 1913, to the delight of Carolyn's friends, many of whom had secretly felt such a turn-around was impossible for the chronically depressed widow.

"She was deeply attached to [Joseph] and mourned his death so keenly that it had not been until lately that her friends thought it was probable that she would marry again," wrote the reporter who covered Carolyn's second marriage.

The fifty-one-year-old prince was a hotelier in his own right, with several properties to his name in Europe. When the couple began to frequent the Mount Washington, the staff there nicknamed Carolyn the "Princess." This particular princess began to spend much of her time in her new husband's native France, but she returned annually to Mount Washington for the summer season. Upon her return, the staff, who loved and respected her, knew she would inspect every corner of the hotel. She would then retire to her private suite, Room 314. She began to entertain frequently at the hotel. It was not unusual in the heat of summer for Carolyn to personally invite fifty friends and guests into her private dining room, now known by everyone at the hotel as the Princess Lounge.

In a departure from her previous morose ways, the Princess would now watch from her hidden balcony as hotel guests came down for dinner. Then, after all had arrived, she would make a grand entrance into the dining hall, assured that she would not be outdressed by even the most fashionable socialite. She also took on some quirks, including her unusual attachment to her intricately carved four-poster bed. The bed and its finely detailed headboard, which Carolyn would order disassembled and shipped via ocean liner to wherever she was staying, is still in use at the hotel today. She also became very active in her adopted country of France. During World War I she volunteered in French hospitals as well as donating time and money to other philanthropies. Following the armistice, she was awarded the Croix de Guerre with palms by the French government for her service.

Alas, the Princess's happiness was short-lived. It lasted through nine years of marriage. Then, as suddenly as she had been left alone the first time, Carolyn de Faucigny-Lucinge was widowed again in 1922. She returned to a life of gray solitude until she died in 1936 in Providence, Rhode Island, at the age of sixty-seven.

Her life of ups and downs, highs and lows, may have come to an end, but the Princess's routine appearances at the Mount Washington Resort were about to increase in earnest. Shortly after Carolyn's funeral, the staff maintaining the hotel through the dormant winter season began reporting strange sightings of the Princess, the woman they knew as Carolyn. At the same time, there came the newly unexplained phenomenon of lights flashing on and off in the hotel towers.

Fred Hollis has been the head of security at the resort for many years. He has seen the magnificent old place shine in many ways while working the 6 p.m. to 2 a.m. shift.

Until fifteen years ago, the storied old hotel was closed during the winter. The water was drained from the pipes to keep them from freezing and the heat was turned off, leaving the Mount Washington at the mercy of the brutal northern New England winter. Despite the biting cold and suffocating dark of the winter nights, conditions that would repel most any living thing, the hotel's owners maintained a security detail on the premises twenty-four hours a day to protect the place. Fred is among the few living souls who have seen the Mount Washington Resort dark, frozen, and empty. It's not a scene for the faint of heart.

"It was six or eight degrees inside the hotel," Fred says. "There were ice crystals on the carpet, and it was like you were walking on egg cartons."

The whitewashed interior walls of the hotel also glimmered with a patina of frost. On clear nights, with the full moon hovering over Crawford Notch, wan moonlight shone through the hundreds of windowpanes, reflecting off the jagged ice crystals and casting eerie, surreal shadows throughout the empty building.

"You could see whatever you wanted to see," Fred says of the strange images that danced through the rooms and hallways on many a lonely New Hampshire night.

Fred was making his rounds alone one night, moving with purpose through the empty old hotel. As part of his duties, he had to key in at twenty-two punch clocks located throughout the hotel as proof that he had completed his inspection duties. He marched across the Mount Washington's massive Grand Ballroom toward the clock on the other side of the hall. The place was dark and deathly silent. Suddenly, near the center of the deserted ballroom, Fred stopped in his tracks.

A wave of steely cold pierced him. Despite a lifetime of winters in New England, it was a cold like he'd never experienced, indoors or out.

"What the hell was that?" he thought to himself.

Fred began to retreat.

"Every single hair was electrified, like they were buzzing," Fred recalls.

Fred made it out of the ballroom and back into the main hallway. The sensation stopped abruptly and never returned.

"I had been in that room hundreds of times before that and thousands of times since then," Fred says. "I had never had that experience, and I've never had it again."

Fred Hollis is not the only person to have experienced the unexplained at the Mount Washington. Not surprisingly, many of the supernatural occurrences take place in Room 314, where guests and employees encounter the ghostly Princess in her favorite suite. The tales range from simple rustling or flapping sheets in Room 314 to other more frightening encounters.

"There seems to be a lot of activity in that room," Fred adds with a great degree of understatement.

One woman, a regular guest of the hotel, was staying in Room 314 one night when she was awakened by a soft but persistent sound.

Tap tap tap tap tap.

Frightened, she lay motionless, barely breathing. The sound came again.

Tap tap tap tap tap.

It was the sound of someone gently tapping on her door. Scared but determined to investigate, she crept quietly across the pitch-black hotel room, feeling her way along one wall. The tapping just outside her guest-room door continued, faint but insistent. She mustered all of her courage and reached for the doorknob. She slid back the security chain and opened the deadbolt. Then she slowly opened the door just enough to peek into the hall.

What she saw frightened her so badly she was unable to even scream.

What she could describe only as a sort of translucent person wrapped in a sheet or shroud was floating in the hall outside her room. The eyes of the specter met hers and the woman's blood ran cold. She was face to face with a ghost in the middle of the night on the third floor of a dark hotel that had suddenly gone as silent as a tomb. Almost against her will, she continued to open the door until it was fully open. The spirit held her gaze for a moment longer, then floated in a translucent blur down the hall and then promptly disappeared.

"Fred, it wasn't my imagination," she later told the security chief, adding that she hadn't touched a drop of alcohol the entire evening. So adamant was she about the tale that Fred says he had no choice but to believe her. The fact that he's had his own eerie experiences there lends credence to her story.

Room 314 has frightened its fair share of others over the years. In one instance, a housekeeper was in the room when she heard noises from the bathroom that would stop as soon as she entered, but resume when she walked out. Since there was only one door into the room, she knew it was impossible that someone was playing a trick on her. So spooked was the woman that she had another housekeeper stay with her until the job was finished.

The Princess, or whatever other spirits inhabit the old hotel, don't limit their activities to Carolyn's old suite—far from it. One late winter evening Fred was on duty when a fellow security guard came up to him and said she had heard a persistent "whirring sound" but couldn't locate the source. Fred at first dismissed the coworker's fears. At the time, the place was an old building with old windows set in a mountain pass in the middle of a New England winter. Things occasionally creaked and moaned.

"You're just hearing the wind," Fred told the other guard.

She was insistent, however. This was not a sound from the wind, she said. It wasn't a natural sound at all. When he saw how convinced and concerned the woman was, Fred agreed to help her check it out. As soon as they started their hunt, Fred heard it too.

"The more you listened, the more it sounded like a melody," Fred remembers.

The pair spent the better part of that winter night searching for the source of the sound. They walked every floor and stairwell of the four-floor monstrosity to find the origin of the sound but, to their dismay and growing uneasiness, found they could never get closer to the source. They also couldn't get any farther away from it. No matter where they were in the vast structure, the volume stayed the same.

In addition to sounds, unexplained aromas have been known to waft through the hotel. Once, with the four-person security team hunkered down in the Mount Washington Hotel, waiting out another cold New Hampshire night, Fred gave the air a sniff and wrinkled his nose in disgust.

"One of the smells I disdain is cigar smoke," he says, recalling the strange incident. "It was the distinct aroma of cigars."

Fred knew that none of the guards smoked. He also knew there wasn't another living soul anywhere near them that night.

"The hotel was kept locked at all times. We'd lock ourselves in," Fred says. "We knew no one else was in there."

So where did the unmistakable scent of cigar smoke come from? Perhaps the ghost of some fat cat, fresh off the back nine and parading through the hotel with stogie in hand. Indeed, there were many such characters in the Mount Washington's heyday. Yankees slugger George Herman "Babe" Ruth polluted his fair share of mountain air with his cigars as he made his way to and from the resort's golf course. Babe loved the course Donald Ross had designed at Mount Washington so much, in fact, he kept a locker in the clubhouse that remains there to this day.

But Babe Ruth would have hardly stood out, as a cigar smoker or a high roller, in the cadre of big names that passed through the resort's halls. F. W. Woolworth, John D. Rockefeller, John Kenneth Galbraith, Christian Barnard, and U.S. Presidents William H. Taft, Woodrow Wilson, and Warren G. Harding all stayed at the resort at one time or another, as did Bob Hope and Rudy Vallee. But if any of the old spirits were likely to leave a trail of cigar smoke in their wake, it's hard to ignore the fact that Winston Churchill, when still a young British journalist in 1906, spent a night in the Mount Washington Hotel. Or perhaps it was one of the dignitaries who for three weeks in July 1944 was part of the Bretton Woods monetary conference. The world was invited to the Mount Washington Hotel via newspapers, radio, and newsreels that covered the gathering, in which 730 delegates from forty-four Allied countries sought to stabilize the world economy through a system of monetary rules, institutions, and procedures. It was there that the groundwork for the International Monetary Fund and the World Bank was laid. Perhaps the cigar smoke was from the ghost of Henry Morgenthau, the elected conference chairman and the secretary of the treasury under President Franklin D. Roosevelt. In front of a bank of microphones, illuminated by hundreds of flashing camera bulbs, he reminded the attendees that a war was still being fought. "As they prosper or perish, the work which we do here will be judged," Morgenthau said.

Since those days, the hotel has undergone a series of renovations, most recently in July 2008, when the wrap-around veranda was restored and amenities such as a spa and additional meeting space were added. And the improvements have not been limited to the hotel; the golf course Babe Ruth was so fond of has been greatly improved since the Sultan of Swat played there.

If Donald Ross's original efforts were poorly executed, at least his work was not in vain. In 2008 the course reopened after a nearly yearlong renovation at the hands of architect Brian Silva, widely considered one of the finest in his field at restoring Ross layouts. Today at Mount Washington, for the first time, Ross's original intent shines in all its intended glory, making it one of the most scenic golf courses in the Northeast, if not all of the United States. Set in a mountain valley, the course gently weaves its way over the 160 acres with only slight elevation changes, a rarity for a mountain course. While playing, golfers looking to the north are entranced by the ominous Mount Washington, sitting high and mighty in the distance looming over every hummock and swale. Perhaps visible is a black puff of smoke from the engine of the Cog Railway during its slow ascent to the summit or a plume of white smoke during its shorter and speedier descent.

A turn to the south reveals the grandeur of the gleaming white hotel capped off with its distinctive crimson roof, built in the Spanish Renaissance Revival style. No matter which way the golfer gazes, he will find it difficult to concentrate on the task at hand.

Silva also restored the old Alex Findlay layout located near the entrance to the hotel, the course Carolyn gazed upon on the day the hotel opened. (It is now nine holes and known as the Panorama course.)

Of all the golfers who have teed up at Mount Washington, only one is commemorated with a plaque: Hank Pella.

"He was a country philosopher," Fred Hollis says, laughing. "He gave out more free advice than good advice."

Hank also, as Dick Hallorann might have put it, "had the shine." He proved himself to be a bit of a seer.

Fred grew up in Rhode Island fishing the plentiful waters of Narragansett Bay and the Sakonnet River before heading north to New Hampshire. During his time at the Mount Washington Resort he has dispensed countless hours of sage advice to young employees looking for direction. He has sat them in what he calls his "therapy chair" to "talk a little shell-fisherman talk."

It was Hank, though, who gave his friend a real lesson.

Some years ago, unbeknownst to anyone at the hotel, Fred and his wife were wracked with worry. They had applied to adopt a boy, the first of ten children they would welcome into their home over the years. But the process had bogged down, and the couple began to think their dream would never come to fruition.

One day Hank walked up to Fred and, for no reason, handed him a card. On one side was a picture of a captain on the bridge of his ship being tossed about in stormy seas and on the other side were the handwritten words: "Keep the faith."

The next day Fred and his wife received word that the adoption had gone through and to this day he carries the card Hank gave him in his wallet.

"I never said a word about the problem," Fred swears.

Was it the hotel or the golf course where he spent so much time that gave Hank the knack for fortune-telling?

Did the Mount Washington make him "shine"? Surely some think the place is just haunted enough to do almost anything. Even those who don't know about the legends of the Princess and have never heard any supernatural tales about the place can be spooked by what happens there.

The hotel hired a carpenter several winters ago to make some repairs during the off-season. The craftsman, working alone, was unaware of any of the ghost stories that swirl about the grand old hotel. He simply went about his work—that is, until the spirits of the Mount Washington intervened.

Whenever the man left the room he was working in, tools would mysteriously move.

"My table saw was right there, and then I go to lunch," the exasperated carpenter told Fred one day. "And then the saw is on the other side of the room. I was working alone; nobody was in the building with me!"

And not just humans are spooked by whatever exists inside the Mount Washington.

Fred remembers the time a hotel employee brought his beloved German shepherd into the hotel one winter evening. The dog, thrilled with the realization it had free run of the place, bolted from the lower lobby up the stairs. Soon afterward, there was the sound of frightened yips, and the dog came charging down the stairs.

"He had his tail between his legs. He beat feet out of the building," Fred says. "From then on that dog would not go back into the hotel."

Who knows what the poor beast saw or detected. Maybe he caught a glimpse of the Princess. Or perhaps the frightened animal caught the scent of some other force that now calls the Mount Washington Hotel home.

Again, the words of Dick Hallorann, the Scatman Crothers character in *The Shining,* come to mind.

"Maybe things that happen leave other kinds of traces behind. Not things that anyone can notice, but things that people who 'shine' can see. I think a lot of things happened right here in this particular hotel over the years. And not all of 'em was good."

Chapter 4

Canton Public Golf Course: The Headless Frenchman

Canton, Connecticut, was an important waypoint between Hartford and Albany dating back to the Revolutionary War. By the time Canton Public Golf Course was built in the 1930s, the place was already thick with stories of murder, mayhem, and a headless French horseman, whose legend actually inspired the golf course's developer.

The autumn night was black as pitch and turning cold as the lone French soldier tied up his horse outside the Horsford Tavern in Canton, Connecticut. He'd been riding since morning heading northwest from Hartford along the old Albany Turnpike on his way to Saratoga, New York, with saddlebags laden with silver and gold. Like many weary travelers who found themselves in the remote stopover town of Canton, in the shadow of Connecticut's Litchfield Hills, he was in desperate need of refreshment and rest.

On this particular fall night in 1777, the Horsford's taproom was packed with regulars buzzing about the Revolution. Word had already reached Canton that a ragtag bunch of American fighters under the direction of Horatio Gates and Benedict Arnold was routing General John Burgoyne's seasoned British forces up in Saratoga. Sensing a change in momentum in the Revolution, a group of French army regulars had recently joined the battle on the side of the colonists.

"Come, sit, tell us what you've seen, my friend," called one of the locals when he saw the young man in French uniform.

The Frenchman sank wearily into a chair and let the heavy saddlebags drop with a metallic jingle to the tavern floor. "You know as much as I, my American brother," the soldier said. "We are giving the British and their bloody mercenaries hell at Freeman's Farm and Bemis Heights."

"We are one in this fight, the Americans and the French!" shouted a patron, and the Horsford erupted in cheering and toasting of the young Frenchman. "You are our brother this night!"

"Indeed we fight together," the French soldier said when the room had quieted. "But the French soldier is not like the American. He fights with his head, not with his heart like the colonists. For him this is work, eh? He must be paid well and on time. And always in cash.

"And so, my friends," he said, poking at the stuffed saddlebags with the point of his boot, "I am on my way to deliver this payroll to ensure our continued success against the British tyrants and the Hessian dogs."

For the rest of the evening, the young Frenchman was the honored guest of the Horsford's regulars; he was a hero and a warrior, a bearer of good news for the independent-spirited colonists of Canton. Near midnight, with his fill of ale and food and good wishes, the French soldier hefted the saddlebags and bid his hosts goodnight. He paid the tavern's owner for a room and staggered his way to the stairs, intent on a good night's sleep before continuing his journey north.

The Frenchman and his saddlebags of silver and gold were never seen again.

When more than a week had passed with no sign of the soldier or the army payroll in Saratoga, French military officials set out to retrace his steps. Suspicions that the soldier might have simply deserted and absconded with the money quickly dissolved when investigators reached Canton and discovered he'd simply vanished without benefit of his horse, which witnesses said remained outside the Horsford for much of the day following his disappearance before being led away by the tavern's owner. Suspicion, therefore, turned to the innkeeper, who had a reputation for violence and criminal behavior.

"I swear to you, he left here in the morning safe and sound," the innkeeper told the French authorities. "I watched him walk out that door as surely as you're standing here."

Unconvinced, but without any evidence, the French investigators left the Horsford Tavern. In the ensuing months, some eyebrows were raised when a Baptist church was built not far from the Horsford without need of a loan. Neither the presiding minister nor his parishioners could explain where the construction money came from, but rumors circulated throughout Canton that the church had been paid for with French gold and silver donated by a guilt-ridden thief.

Still, the exact fate of the French paymaster might have remained a mystery forever, if not for a fire several years later that gutted the old inn. The blaze and its aftermath brought out a number of Canton residents who spent days picking over the charred rubble of the tavern, looking for souvenirs and valuables. Two young boys were pulling apart the former sleeping quarters, picking up doorknobs and brass hinges, when suddenly one began shouting.

"Hey! Over here! Oh, horrors! Horrors! It's a dead man," screamed the boy. "A dead man with no head!"

The shouts attracted several nearby adults, who ran to see what gruesome thing the lads had uncovered. Indeed, the boys had found the skeletal remains of a young man, minus his skull, secreted in the Horsford's walls.

"I suppose we'll never have to wonder again," remarked one old Yankee dryly, "what ever happened to that young Frenchman and his bags of gold."

Most felt the mysterious disappearance had been solved. For the few who still doubted, however, the ghost of the French paymaster began to deliver more spectral proof.

Within weeks of the discovery of the body, reliable Canton residents began to report sightings of a headless horseman aboard a fire-eyed steed running recklessly at full gallop on the Albany Turnpike. The ghost always appeared in the same spot, a place one nineteenth-century historian described as "where the trees shadow the road so completely that no sunlight penetrates even at midday." The ghost was always traveling northwest, toward Saratoga, his long cape flowing behind his headless body. The sudden appearance of the decapitated demon speeding along on a mount with glowing eyes became infamous in Canton for spooking horses, causing them to throw their riders or send their carriages careening into the woods.

Sightings of Canton's headless rider continued for the next 150 years and were the stuff of local legend by the time a young James E. Lowell stood on the banks of Cherry Pond and began plotting his future in earnest. Lowell skipped stones across the glass-smooth surface of the pond and tried to imagine a way to sell people on the beauty, the serenity, and perhaps even the mystery of this hidden treasure in the New England countryside.

Just a few years before, the studious young James had been raising chickens and selling eggs from his family's farm in the central Connecticut town of Meriden, but he wanted more. After a few visits to the Farmington River Valley—and a few recountings of the headless-ghost story—he became sure his future was in Canton and convinced his parents to make the move. They bought Higley Farm, which included the land around Cherry Pond. They lived there for a time, but their fascination with the remote Canton outpost was short-lived. Though James thrived in the rural setting, James's mother, Charlotte, missed the bustle of Meriden, a thriving mill town known for its silver-plating factories. Over their son's protests, the Lowells rented out the Higley place and moved back to Meriden. James finished high school in Canton, then went on to Dean Academy and Dartmouth College, where an economics professor changed the way he looked at the world at large, and the farm in Canton in particular.

"If you feed or entertain the people," the professor told young James Lowell, "you'll never lose your job."

And so, his studies finished, James Lowell found himself back on Higley Farm, back on the shores of Cherry

Pond in Canton, the words of his teacher echoing in his head.

"Entertain the people."

Maybe it was while watching the ripples dissipate along the placid surface of the pond that it came to him in a flash.

"Golf," Lowell might have thought. "And ghosts. Of course! We'll entertain the people straight out of their wits."

It was settled. James Lowell would build a golf course in the beautiful, natural setting in Canton. He would finance course construction by selling lakefront house lots, and he would promote his development with the fascinating tales of the supernatural that already swirled around the place.

The first thing James Lowell did was take advantage of the fact of the unfortunate French paymaster's demise. He changed the name of Cherry Pond to Secret Lake, claiming the boots of the dead man were found in the lake, hoping to capitalize on the grisly story and its mysterious, supernatural aftermath. Before long, the parcels were sold and the nine-hole Canton Public Golf Course was built on the old Higley Farm property, opening on Memorial Day 1932. The 3,068-yard, par-36 course was designed by Robert J. Ross, a Connecticut native. Until it closed in 2003, it lay along the Albany Turnpike, now known as Route 44, in a golf-rich area that also includes the nearby Farmington Woods Country Club and the Golf Club of Avon. It also sat within sight of the spot "where no sunlight penetrates even at midday;" the favorite haunt of Canton's famed headless rider.

James Lowell went on to become an influential member in Connecticut politics, serving as chairman first of the state's dairy and fruit commission and then of the finance commission before working his way up to state representative. But if Lowell thought the ghostly happenings around Canton were merely a convenient marketing tool for his golf community, the spirits of the Litchfield Hills would prove him wrong. As subsequent generations of the Lowell family can attest, there really are supernatural forces at work around Canton, and the headless ghost of a young French soldier may not be alone among them. Indeed, Canton Public Golf Course had its very own ghostly tales.

The haunted happenings around the course began in earnest when James Lowell's son, Walter, took over management of the facility in 1956. James Lowell and his wife continued to live in the property's main farmhouse. Walter and his young wife, Phyllis, would be working in the course's pro shop, located in the basement of an old barn on the property, so Walter decided to turn the barn into a two-story apartment. Walter quickly found himself serving not only as Canton's superintendent and golf professional, but as its unofficial ghost hunter as well.

During the renovations, workers discovered that the farmhouse his parents now occupied once had served as a tavern and inn, much like the Horsford. For those weary travelers unable or unwilling to pay the room rates, the second floor of the barn had proved a convenient place to crawl off and get some sleep. Indeed, the place being turned into a home for newlyweds Walter and Phyllis Lowell once had been a sort of country flophouse. As far back as pre–Civil War times, transients and hobos often took shelter in the barn. Recurring guests included Jules Bourglay, better known as the Leatherman, a legendary leather-clad French drifter who wandered through New York and Connecticut from the early 1860s until the late 1880s in a 365-mile circular route that took thirty-four days to complete. During the renovations, Walter also found fifty-year-old hay-stuffed mattresses used by workers who had helped build the Canton Public Course by day and holed up in the barn by night. What went on in the barn all those years, one can only guess. If most of the lodgers were honorable and well-intentioned, there was sure to be the occasional unsavory character who bunked there as well.

With the bulk of the detritus cleared, Walter and Phyllis moved into the new barn apartment in early 1957 with Brownie, their small, spirited beagle with all the heart of a German shepherd.

Despite the hound's squat stature, Walter saw Brownie as a sort of unlikely watchdog. "He would take on a bear if he had to," Walter says of his beagle, with a laugh. And indeed, the dog had proved his mettle around the golf course more than once. When a rabid fox attacked several golf course employees, Brownie charged the snarling, feral beast, grabbing it by the hind leg and holding on until Walter could put it down.

So it was disquieting for Walter and Phyllis, shortly after they settled into their new home, to confront a force at Canton that not even Brownie dared tangle with.

Walter was feeling on edge one March night. He couldn't say why. It was just one of those late-winter evenings, especially cold, dark, and still, that left him feeling something was amiss—or soon would be. He, Phyllis, and Brownie were lounging around the first floor of the apartment. The noise above their heads started low, like an indistinct, distant rumble. Brownie noticed it too, ears perking up, head cocked, straining to listen.

Thump. Grrrrrrrt. Thump. Grrrrrrrt. Thump. Grrrrrrrt.

It grew louder and clearer as it moved across the floor directly overhead. The thud of a leather boot on pine floorboards was followed by the dragging of a bum leg.

Thump. Grrrrrrrt. Thump. Grrrrrrrt.

The couple and their dog stood paralyzed with fear. Brownie snapped out of it first and ran under the television to hide.

Sure there was an intruder in the house, Walter grabbed his .22 pistol and charged upstairs. He threw on the lights. The second floor was empty.

He returned to the living room. The noise had moved outside to the porch. Suddenly the door flew open. Despite the stillness of the evening, Phyllis was immediately enveloped in a blast of cold wind.

"Whatever was there just came by us into the living room," she told Walter as she raced to close and lock the door. Brownie, as brave as he was, remained under the television, too frightened to venture out from his hiding spot.

The incident was just the first in a string of unexplained happenings visited upon Walter and Phyllis at the Canton Public Golf Course. The couple frequently awoke to find doors leading to the porch—doors they'd been sure to lock the night before—wide open. Doors would even swing open while Walter and Phyllis were sitting at the dinner table or relaxing in the living room. The frequent occurrences unnerved the newlyweds so much that they attached slide bolts to all the doors.

The door openings abated, but the cold spells and the odd feelings continued. About a year later, the noisy visitor with the bad leg returned. It was on a similarly dark, cold March night that the Lowells once again heard the thumping and dragging sound coming from the room above. Walter raced upstairs, snapping on all the lights.

"We're living here now," Walter bellowed into the empty room. "You're welcome anytime you want to come, but we're not leaving."

He waited for a response but got none. Apparently, however, Walter's words made an impact. The ghost was never heard from again.

The Lowells lived in the apartment at the golf course for five more years without bother before moving to a house down the road. A family friend took over the apartment for a number of years, after which Walter's mother moved in. Neither ever heard footsteps, felt a cold wind, or saw locked doors fling open. In fact, Walter's tales were routinely dismissed by everyone in the Lowell family.

"Nobody knows anything about it. They think I'm crazy," a frustrated Walter said to Phyllis.

She responded with a knowing glance and a smile. They knew what they had heard, felt, and seen. And after all, Walter thought, his father had built the course and the housing development on the premise that Cherry Pond was Secret Lake, a place tainted by the long-ago murder of a French paymaster who became Canton's famous headless ghost. If the spirits wanted to exact some commission for their part in helping to sell James Lowell's golf community, who could blame them?

Chapter 5

Leatherstocking Golf Course: The Otesaga Hotel's Unwanted Guests

The Otesaga Resort of Cooperstown, New York, with its wonderful golf course, dates back only to the first decade of the 1900s. Located in a region made famous by James Fenimore Cooper's Leatherstocking Tales, the Otesaga, however, has more than its share of stories—ghost stories.

Even on a bright summer's day, the Otesaga Resort's massive Federal-style brick facade and towering thirty-foot columns strike an imposing figure. In the dead of the New York winter, with the wind howling off a frozen Otsego Lake, the place turns downright otherworldly. Shadows dance across row after row of darkened windows staring blindly from the empty hotel. Glider swings lined up on the 180-foot-long porch sway without rhythm or reason. Chains securing the racks of canoes and paddleboats along the resort's lakefront rattle and creak like tortured demons in the biting cold.

None of which bothers Bill June much.

Buzz-cut and barrel-chested with a bone-cracking handshake and an intolerance for tomfoolery, Bill has spent the past twenty years as the Otesaga's night watchman. He patrols the grounds, from the hotel to the docks to the

Leatherstocking Golf Course, every day from 4 p.m. to midnight, even in the cold, dark winter months. Bill sees it as his responsibility to guard well the Cooperstown, New York, resort property sixty miles southwest of Albany. When the place is shut down for the long winter season, his job is to keep all non-employees out. Everyone—living or dead.

It was just such a forbidding winter night two years ago when Bill June heard a sound overhead in the otherwise suffocating silence of what should have been an empty hotel. Bill went up the front stairway to the third floor to investigate. He sent a fellow watchman up the back stairs just in case.

Stepping into the dim, third-floor hallway, Bill saw the couple about thirty yards away, walking away from him. The woman was dressed "in a ballroom gown, the kind you would go dancing in," Bill says. The man wore tails as black as pitch. Bill started after them, but before he could catch up, the couple had gone down the back stairway. They were gone.

Bill's coworker arrived at the top of the stairway down which the ghostly pair had made their escape. But Bill knew what he'd say. The other night watchman had seen nothing, encountered no one. "I sent him up that stairwell and he never met anybody," Bill says, chagrined. "It made me feel kind of foolish."

And foolish is not a feeling Bill June is comfortable with. In addition to his job at the hotel, he runs a nuisance-animal control business and works for the state and the county. He grew up in Doodleville, New York, a village that was abandoned in the late 1960s when the mines shut down and was later absorbed into Bear Mountain State Park. As tough and serious as he is, Bill won't be dissuaded from what he's seen in his two decades at the Otesaga.

"I don't want anyone making a mockery of what I say. I don't say what I don't know for a fact," he says bluntly.

And he knows for a fact he's seen the well-heeled couple, or the man by himself, at least three times since he started at the Otesaga in 1987. He can't describe their faces. "They always turn away from me," he says. But he knows their clothing by heart. That formal dress worn by the mysterious spirit strolling the hallways during Bill's winter rounds hearkens back to the turn-of-the-century grandeur of the resort once called the O-Te-Sa-Ga Hotel.

The luxury hotel and golf course located on the southern tip of Otsego Lake was the brainchild of brothers Edward S. and Steven C. Clark, who hoped a world-class resort would revive the economically depressed Cooperstown region. When the plans were first announced, one local newspaper said the news "was received with great joy by the people of Cooperstown, and flags were displayed all along Main Street during the afternoon." Thirty years before the Baseball Hall of Fame was built in the town, one resident said the O-Te-Sa-Ga would be "more of benefit to Cooperstown than anything else that could happen."

In early 1908, the Clark brothers bought the Holt-Averill estate, which included seven hundred feet of shoreline on Lake Otsego. The crystal-clear lake serves as the headwaters for the Susquehanna River. It seemed to the Clarks the perfect place for their dream resort, a place to attract the rich and famous from New York City and beyond. James Fenimore Cooper made the region famous with his Leatherstocking Tales, including *The Last of the Mohicans*, in which he called the body of water Glimmerglass.

In *The Deerslayer,* Cooper called Otsego Lake "a broad sheet of water, so placid and limpid, that it resembled a bed of the pure mountain atmosphere."

Some 150 workers descended on the Holt-Averill property, tore down a century-old house on the property, and, in less than sixteen months, built much of what still stands as the spectacular Otesaga Resort Hotel. The facility opened with much fanfare on July 13, 1909. Today there are nearly 250 rooms, and the famed twenty-foot-wide porch still wraps around the north side of the hotel, offering a panoramic view of the lake and the undeveloped hills on the far shore.

Then, as today, the Otesaga offered many activities for its wealthy guests. There was golf on a nine-hole course designed by eminent architect Devereux Emmet, fantastic bass fishing, sailing, swimming, croquet, and hiking in the unspoiled nearby mountains or around the lake. The golf course was expanded to eighteen holes a few years later, with the 18th green sitting just below the hotel, nuzzled up against the lake, giving relaxing vacationers a wonderful view of golfers playing the final, testing hole.

There was also fine dining, with French-trained A. C. Bono in the role of head chef. The first meal was a luncheon featuring Potage O-te-sa-ga, canapé caviar, consommé Salferino, potatoes Parisienne, breaded lamb chops, boiled halibut, banana fritters, rhubarb pie, cherries, raisins, figs, and dates. The large, well-trained staff was overseen by J. D. Price, who'd held similar positions at Mount Washington and Mount Pleasant Houses at Bretton Woods in New Hampshire. Indeed, the Clarks provided every amenity their guests could desire at such a grand getaway.

But something other than relaxation and recreation came with the Clark brothers' resort and golf course.

It has become known as the kind of place where a waitress sent to check on customers on the veranda might come running back deathly pale and spooked. In one such case, a panicked and breathless server told coworkers that as she walked along the porch, she came up behind a man in a rocking chair. As she approached to see if he needed a drink, she looked down to flip open her order pad, then back up to see an empty chair still gently rocking back and forth.

No one is sure when the first sightings took place, but for decades now, the Otesaga has been haunted by a variety of restless, often playful spirits. Mostly the staff has experienced the phenomena, but guests, too, have been spooked by unexplained noises, apparitions, sensations of unseen presences, sudden chills in otherwise warm rooms, and sweet music floating through the Otesaga's crisp, pine-tinged air. For a place with a remarkable number of supernatural encounters, however, there are precious few theories as to their origin. There are rumors of a suicide in the resort more than fifty years ago, but other than that, no tales of murders or other tragic deaths at the Otesaga exist.

Still, there have been all manner of eerie events there.

In 2000, the Otesaga's current owner, Jane Clark, moved the elderly residents of Thanksgiving Home, a Cooperstown nursing home she also owned, into the hotel's west wing while the health care facility was being renovated. The elderly patients ended up staying in the Otesaga longer than expected when a fire destroyed Thanksgiving Home just weeks before it was to reopen.

One evening, one of Jane Clark's nurses approached Bill June. She wanted to know if the resort had anyone who was playing a music box. "I told her no, but I had heard it," Bill recalls, chuckling. "She said, 'What do you mean you've heard it?'"

Bill knew that for years, gentle, bell-like music had wafted throughout the second floor, though its source could never be found. The young nurse was incredulous but admitted to Bill that she'd heard the music so clearly "she could do the tune for me."

Not all of the Otesaga's ghostly encounters have been frightening. The spirits at the resort also have a sense of humor. Once, while Bill was talking to a woman at the front desk, he felt as though someone had grabbed his behind.

"If I knew they were going to do that, I would have backed up," he said out loud, startling the woman he was chatting with. She never doubted that Bill surely felt something.

Except for sharing his ghost stories with fellow employees who need to know what to expect in and around the Otesaga, Bill rarely talks about the encounters. He never brings them up with family or friends. He keeps the stories to himself. Like the time he was patrolling the parking lot in the dead of winter and glanced up at the empty hotel only to see a woman looking out a window toward the golf course. Or the time he heard music drifting from the hotel's unoccupied west wing. He's not scared or spooked by the sightings; Bill just does not want his integrity diminished. He simply tells what he knows.

So do dozens of other Otesaga employees past and present who have witnessed the mysterious and supernatural there.

Janeen Whelan has worked at the resort for more than seven years, mostly as a bartender. She'd long heard the stories of the unexplained but had no real encounters of her own until several recent, unsettling experiences. Janeen was heading downstairs to the hotel's Hawkeye Lounge. As she walked, she scanned the glass display cases that line the walls. In addition to showing off items of significance in the Otesaga's history, the reflective glass panes offer a preview of what is around the corner.

"You can see someone coming down the hallway; you can see them before actually seeing them," Janeen says. "I saw a man. I saw his face. I turned the hallway to say hello and there was nothing there."

Not long after, Janeen was making her way down a hall-way on the same floor when she glanced into a sitting room. She noticed a man sitting alone in the room. Grabbing her pad, she turned into the room to take his order. But when Janeen looked up, she was stunned to find she was alone.

"I went to wait on him and nothing was there; nothing was in the room."

Her most disturbing supernatural encounter came late one night in 2007. The door leading from the Hawkeye into the adjacent Templeton Lounge was locked. Suddenly, some-one or something started vigorously rattling the handle. Frightened but determined to prove to herself there was nothing to fear, nerves on end, she wanted to believe that there was no ghost—probably just a hotel patron looking for one last cocktail.

"I said, 'OK, I'm going to go and see, so I know people are there and I will not be freaked out,'" she says, shivering at the unnerving memory. "And nothing was there."

That was the last night Janeen closed up the Hawk-eye on her own. Unlike the Otesaga's gruff night watchman, Janeen is decidedly spooked by her ghostly experiences, shivering at some of her own recollections. When she works late now, she always has another employee with her. "I get the worst feeling. I feel like if I turn around, I'm going to see someone. Every time I close up, my heart is pounding out of my chest."

She's not alone.

Waitress Tricia Simonds and waiter Dave Golden were dropping off the night's take in the office behind the hotel's front desk late one evening. The pair turned a corner, walked into the office, and were met by a bone-chillingly cold presence, even though all the windows were closed.

"You know 'fight or flight'? I wanted to run away," Dave says. "She was the brave one and wanted to stay."

The ghosts of the Otesaga also like to be on a first-name basis with the staff.

Rachel Purcell Donnelly was working a crowded cocktail hour in the hotel's Glimmer Glass Room a few years ago when she heard someone call her name. The voice was neither male nor female, and it spoke her name in a soothing tone, like a mother gently waking her child from a deep sleep.

"I turned around; nobody was near me," she says.

The experience would happen many more times. "Usually when nobody was around," she adds. Janeen and Tricia also encountered the soft-spoken, name-calling ghost, and always with the same result. The women turned to see who beckoned and found no one there.

But if hearing her name called softly by an invisible force was mildly disturbing, Rachel's encounter with the Otesaga's mysterious swapping elevators was downright spooky. She was working in the Hawkeye bar on the ground floor near the end of the night shift when the bartender sent her up to the veranda to collect the remaining empty glasses, which she did without incident.

Heading back down to the bar, she got into the right-hand elevator, but when she arrived at the ground floor she came out on the left-hand side.

"I told my assistant manager what happened," she says. "He wasn't surprised."

Turns out he had his own experience.

Late on a winter night at closing time, the hotel was shut up tight for the season, all except for the bar at the Hawk-eye. It was past closing time and the manager was counting the evening's take when he looked up as the night security guard walked past the window on his rounds around the outside of the hotel and the two exchanged silent hellos. A few minutes later, the manager noticed both elevator lights on, indicating both lifts were in use. But the only other person on the property was still outside. The elevators continued to go up and down unabated for the next few minutes before stopping as suddenly as they had started.

Rachel's husband, Sean Donnelly, worked at the Otesaga's Leatherstocking course, where the closest he has come to any paranormal experience are the frightening golf swings he sees regularly. But he's heard enough about Rachel's ghostly encounters to make him believe the hotel is indeed haunted, and he gives an understanding nod as she recounts her tales.

Spooky encounters with spirits aren't limited to the hotel's staff. Four years ago, a couple staying on the third floor called to complain of children running in the hall. A security guard was dispatched only to find the hallway silent. A few minutes later, the couple called again with the same complaint. Sensing a practical joke on the part of some devious adolescents, two security guards were sent up each of the two flights of stairs while a third stayed behind and watched the elevators. Again, nothing was found on the third floor. And again, the couple called soon after to complain. This time the desk person asked them to look outside their door and report what they saw. When the couple looked for themselves, the hallway was empty and silent. Several other guests have since reported similar unexplained disturbances in the Otesaga's halls.

In fact, the Otesaga's hallways were once filled with the sounds of running children—some five decades before those third-floor guests had their mysterious, noisy encounter. Some speculate those running children may be the spirits of former students who have come back to the Otesaga to relive the carefree days of their youth. From 1920 to 1954, the hotel was home to the Knox School for Girls. At that point in the hotel's history, the vacation season was only two months and the girls arrived after the last guest had checked out, and the school year ended well before the first seasonal guest signed the register. The school was forced out of Briarcliff Manor, thirty miles north of New York City, when a fire destroyed the place in 1920. In the school's initial year at the hotel, 162 girls were enrolled, taught by thirty-eight faculty members and cared for by fifty house employees. The students focused on classical studies, music, art, domestic arts, and athletics. The school had a gymnasium and an equestrian club that staged an annual horse show for the Cooperstown residents. The girls also staged a winter carnival and festival on the frozen Otsego Lake.

If most of the Otesaga's hauntings seem largely innocent and mischievous, others have made folks question whether the resort's spirits might also have a temper. In the spring of 2007, Jane Clark—granddaughter and grandniece of the original founders—made a visit to the hotel and asked that a set of chandeliers be cleaned. Less than half an hour later, while an employee was delicately dusting the hundreds of intricate glass pieces on the chandelier in the Glimmer Glass Room, it crashed to the floor, falling from where it had been safely attached since the hotel opening nearly a century earlier.

No one can explain why some who work at the Otesaga have the haunted experiences and others do not. For Bill June, the answer to his rare talent for touching, and being touched by, those in the afterlife might lie in the fact that he died twice in a three-year period and was resuscitated by the same person both times.

When he was eight, Bill was at 10-Foot, a popular swimming hole in Doodleville, when he slipped off a ledge and into the water. When his brother-in-law, Luther Stalter Sr., pulled him out, Bill was not breathing. Luther applied mouth-to-mouth until Bill came to.

"Learn anything?" Luther asked when Bill opened his eyes.

Three years later, while working on a roof with family members, Bill slipped off of the building, slamming his head on a cement step. This time his breathing and heart stopped. Bill was rushed to the hospital in a family car while Luther performed CPR the entire way, getting Bill's breathing and heart started by the time they reached the emergency room.

Since then, Bill has had supernatural encounters away from the Otesaga as well. Like the time he was in his own home with two friends and smelled smoke, even though there was no fire burning at his place. He decided to trek down to his mother's house, where he found her and a friend sound asleep and a log that had rolled out of the wood stove smoldering on the floor.

"I'm not afraid of death and I'm not afraid of dying," Bill says without a hint of doubt or braggadocio in his gravelly voice. "I don't think I've ever been afraid of anything."

He sure isn't afraid of the ghosts he's seen at the Otesaga. In fact, rather than send chills up his spine, the spirits get his blood to boiling. The way Bill sees it, if he can't keep the ghosts off the resort property, he's failing in his night watchman's duties.

"If these people are getting away with this, then they're doing what they're doing better than I'm doing my job," he says, chagrined. "I don't like it. I really don't."

Chapter 6

Biltmore Hotel and Resort: The Gangster Ghost

The fabulously posh Biltmore Hotel in Coral Gables, Florida, has played host to the rich and famous for decades, thanks in part to a gem of a Donald Ross championship course. But it's the ghost of a tubby New York gangster with a taste for cigars and beautiful blondes that has come to define the opulent South Florida retreat.

Thomas "Fatty" Walsh couldn't believe his luck. He pulled his hat brim down a bit against the glaring Florida sunshine and stood on the edge of the world's largest swimming pool, marveling at the beauty, both natural and man-made, of the extravagant Biltmore Hotel.

"If we gotta be on the lam, I could think of worse places," Fatty told his buddy Arthur Clark, with a slap on the back. "Artie, my boy, I think we're home!"

Here in Coral Gables, Florida, Fatty and Arthur would be far removed from constant questioning of the New York City detectives who were pretty sure the pair had a hand in murdering their boss, mob kingpin Arnold Rothstein. They had rolled into South Florida in the spring of 1928 and rented an apartment. And now Fatty and Arthur had come to the area's toniest hotel on a Sunday morning to meet a guy they were told ran the rackets in town.

"You bums stand out like a couple of sore thumbs," shouted Edward Wilson. Eddie came striding out of the Biltmore pool house in a Cuban shirt, straw hat, and shorts. He greeted the two buttoned-down New York mobsters with hugs and kisses. "We gotta get you some clothes, Fatty. You're in the tropics now."

"Nice to meet you too, Eddie," Fatty said, chuckling. All three walked toward the Biltmore's main entrance.

Indeed, Fatty Walsh had found pretty sweet digs. Coral Gables was a long way from the gritty Morrisania section of the Bronx, where Fatty had grown up with a host of other street toughs who made a living making trouble. He'd spent time as a bodyguard to Arnold Rothstein. He'd worked with the most infamous people in his trade—Meyer Lansky, Jack "Legs" Diamond, Charles "Lucky" Luciano, Dutch Schultz. Heck, he'd even been there when Rothstein, whom everyone called Mr. Big, put the fix on the 1919 World Series and, in the process, turned the Chicago White Sox into the infamous Black Sox . He'd been around. But as he followed Eddie and Arthur into the cavernous Biltmore lobby, he looked up in awe at the towering marble columns topped with huge, Moorish arches. He ran a thick finger along the hand-carved wooden wainscoting. He couldn't believe his luck.

"It's like a church in here," Fatty said. Then, seeing two young women approaching the entrance, he ran back to the door and opened it with all the flourish of a Manhattan doorman.

"Good Sunday morning, ladies," Fatty said with a wink and a disarming smile. "Welcome to my hotel." The women sauntered past, giggling at Fatty's flirtations.

"Geez, this guy. Always with the dames," Eddie said to Arthur.

"Only the blondes," Artie replied.

"Hey, Casanova," Eddie shouted, "let's go. It's showtime!"

And in fact, everything about the Biltmore smacked of showtime. The magnificent hotel was the product of the genius of land developer George E. Merrick, the same man who created the city of Coral Gables, a meticulously planned residential community of opulent Mediterranean homes, broad, banyan-lined streets, and lush golf courses. Just four years before Fatty Walsh rolled into town, much of Coral Gables had existed only in the mind of the young Merrick, who also founded the University of Miami. As part of his community development plans, Merrick decided he needed to build "a great hotel . . . which would not only serve as a hostelry to the crowds which were thronging to Coral Gables but also would serve as a center of sports and fashion." Merrick teamed up with hotel magnate John Bowman to develop a resort surrounded by one of the jewels of South Florida golf. In 1925, Donald Ross designed the Biltmore's eighteen-hole championship course. The par-71 course features ample fairways and few bunkers but adds the challenge of Ross's legendary undulating greens.

With the 276-room hotel, world-class golf course, and record-setting 700,000 gallon swimming pool in place, the Biltmore opened to the public in January 1926. The gala debut featured chartered "Miami Biltmore Special" trains to carry the first guests from across the northern United States down to South Florida's hottest new destination. The crowds were awed when the Biltmore's three-hundred-foot, copper-clad tower, a duplicate of the famed Giralda Tower in Seville, Spain, was lit for the first time. At a grand opening party in the stunning Beaux Arts–style Biltmore Country Club building just west of the hotel, popular preacher and newspaper columnist Dr. Frank Crane presided.

"Many people will come and go," Dr. Crane told the crowd, "but this structure will remain a thing of lasting beauty."

And right he was for many years. Despite the looming depression and Prohibition, the Biltmore rarely lacked enthusiastic patrons looking for a taste of the flapper-era high life. Over at the golf course, the living was just as good. In 1926, Bobby Jones, Tommy Armour, Leo Diegel, and Gene Sarazen played in a three-day exhibition match dubbed the Fiesta of the American Tropics. Baseball legend Babe Ruth was also a regular on the course, teeing it up with New York governor and presidential hopeful Al Smith.

The place had a dark side from the beginning, however. Even as the rich and powerful were still learning their way around the sprawling, 150-acre Biltmore property, death and mystery visited the place. In 1927 a wealthy Irishman came to America to invest in new business. He and his dog, a faithful Welsh corgi, took a room at the Biltmore, where he began making deals and sending money home to his wife. But several months into his stay in Coral Gables, the man vanished. His wife, after weeks of no word from her husband, traveled to America to investigate.

When she arrived at the Biltmore, she was greeted outside the main doors by her husband's dog, who seemed to be running loose and extremely agitated. The dog sped off toward the golf course and the woman followed. There, barely concealed in a heap of oak leaves and palm fronds just off the 8th fairway, was the body of her husband. The woman fell to her knees and began to clear the debris covering the body. She made another gruesome discovery: a lump of bloody, matted tan fur. It was the body of her husband's faithful dog, buried beside him. When she looked around, the dog that had led her to the grisly scene had disappeared.

The bad impression that an unsolved murder and a ghostly dog might have had on a lesser hotel couldn't touch the Biltmore, however. The entire place was being fueled by jazz-age splendor and the appetites of the super rich. So it was into this still-new environment of luxury and excess that a rotund, streetwise, cigar-chomping wiseguy named Fatty Walsh landed by virtue of his connections and a bit of luck.

As Walsh rode the elevator with Eddie and Arthur that Sunday morning, he noticed his host had pushed the button for the thirteenth floor.

"They got a thirteenth floor here?" Fatty asked. "I thought that was some sort of bad luck or something. I never saw no hotel with a thirteenth floor."

"Fatty, relax," Eddie cooed. "There's nothing but good luck in this place."

Eddie told his new friends how the Biltmore was always flush with high rollers. Presidents, royalty, and famous stars all wandered the halls, lounged by the pool, and played golf at the resort with regularity.

"Nothing but good luck," Eddie repeated and the elevator doors opened onto the thirteenth floor. The three stared into a very large, vacant room. Arthur and Fatty looked around nervously.

"What da hell is this?" Fatty snapped.

"This," said Eddie, "is the hottest spot south of Philly. By ten o'clock tonight there'll be so many tuxedos and evening dresses in here, you won't be able to move."

He had Fatty's attention now.

"They'll be playing cards and shooting craps and listening to the jazz," Eddie continued. "And they'll be drinking bootleg liquor. Lots and lots of bootleg liquor. In the morning we pack it all up and the next night it starts all over again. Every night. Night after night. I've got this entire floor and the one above it leased out.

"You're just the partner I need to keep this little enterprise going," Eddie told Fatty.

"A speakeasy and a gambling joint?" asked Fatty. "What about the cops?"

"I got them all covered. Politicians, too. They're all in on it. I'm telling you, there's nothing but good luck here."

Eddie told Fatty and Arthur to go explore the hotel and the golf course. He'd set them up with complimentary rooms. Relax, settle in, get a feel for the place, he said. Get ready for a night of drinking, gambling, and schmoozing with Miami's upper crust.

Fatty was pretty much sold already, but he took Eddie up on the offer and went downstairs to check out his new place of business. On the grand veranda, a swinging orchestra was laying down sweet jazz numbers. Families gathered around the massive pool to watch the Water Show, an odd combination of synchronized swimmers, bathing beauties, and alligator wrestling that marked this and every Sunday afternoon at the Biltmore. And everywhere, beautiful blondes, Fatty's biggest weakness.

As Fatty got closer, the music stopped and a barker began to shout, drawing the crowd closer.

"Come see, folks! Come see!" the barker shouted. "High above your heads, it's the boy wonder, Jackie Ott! Come see, folks!"

Fatty looked up. On a tiny platform, nine stories above the pool, a skinny kid waved and hammed it up for the crowd. This was Jackie Ott, son of Alexander Ott, the guy who organized the Water Shows.

"'Boy wonder'?" Fatty thought.

Suddenly the crowd around him howled and cheered as the kid made a perfect swan dive from the dizzying height into the pool. He was immediately surrounded by a cadre of female swimmers moving in rhythm as the band struck up another raucous number.

"Maybe the place is full of luck," thought Fatty.

Within six months, Thomas "Fatty" Walsh was indistinguishable from the high-class clientele of the outlaw casino and speakeasy he and Eddie now ran. Just as Eddie had said, the place was filled to the rafters every night with men in black tie and women dressed to the nines with pearls, cloche hats, and Mary Jane shoes. Fatty sauntered through the crowd with a cigar clenched in his teeth, flirting with the women and rubbing elbows with the richest, most powerful men in the nation. Everybody drank and danced. They gambled on everything, including the outcomes of some spirited skins games being played on the hotel's magnificent golf course. Life at the Biltmore was good.

Until it turned bad.

By early 1929, Eddie and Fatty were more often arguing than glad-handing in the Biltmore's gaming rooms. There were accusations of cheating and skimming. But the final fight between the crime partners was, like many things in Fatty's life, likely over a woman. On an exceptionally muggy evening in March 1929, the casino was packed with 150 guests, who were stunned into silence when Eddie and Fatty began fighting on a balcony off the fourteenth floor.

Clearly agitated, a red-faced Fatty squeezed his portly frame down the narrow spiral staircase back down into the thirteenth-floor casino. Eddie was hot on his heels.

"You're no good, Edward Wilson!" Fatty shouted, punctuating the words with thrusts of his meaty fist in front of the shocked crowd. He turned over one of the card tables in a rage.

Eddie pulled a gun and fired twice at Fatty. Arthur Clark, who was never far from Fatty's side, jumped in to protect his friend and took one shot to the gut for his trouble. As the guests stood huddled in stunned silence, Eddie bolted from the hotel. Police arrived but found the Biltmore's stairwells locked and its elevators shut down, part of Eddie's system for concealing the illegal activity on the thirteenth floor. By the time police made it upstairs, the room was cleared of guests and pretty much everything else. No remnants of the gaming tables or bootleg booze remained. The two responding officers found only Fatty Walsh lying dead on the floor of an empty room, his buddy Arthur badly wounded at his side.

True to his word, Eddie did have law enforcement in his pocket. The Dade County District Attorney had Eddie spirited off to Havana, where he was never heard from again. Arthur Clark recovered from the gunshot wound but likewise faded away for good.

But Fatty Walsh would not go away so easily. He's been at the Biltmore ever since.

The ghost of Fatty Walsh has seen his adopted home through significant ups and downs since the glory days of the '20s and '30s. The hotel played host to the likes of Al Capone, Ginger Rogers, Judy Garland, Bing Crosby, and any number of Roosevelts and Vanderbilts as it became known as part of Miami's "American Riviera." Johnny Weissmuller, the actor best known for playing Tarzan, was once a swimming instructor at the Biltmore. He set a swimming record in the pool before being fired for running naked through the hotel one evening. Weissmuller's ouster lasted only one day, however, when female guests intervened on his behalf and management relented.

At the country club, 1931 saw the inaugural Miami-Biltmore–Coral Gables Open. With $10,000 in prize money, it was the richest tournament in golf at the time. Greats such as Walter Hagen, Paul Runyan, Ralph Guldahl, "Wild" Bill Mehlhorn, and Billy Burke competed in the event, with Gene Sarazen taking the Biltmore title four times.

By the time Sarazen hosted the cup there for the fourth time, however, the shine on the Biltmore Hotel and the Biltmore Country Club was dulling. By the end of World War II, the glory days of the resort had truly passed. The building was taken over by the Department of Defense, which blocked up many of the windows, laid gray linoleum over the marble floors, and opened an Army–Air Force hospital serving wounded and aging veterans there until 1968. The place also served as an annex to the University of Miami's medical school, with a morgue and autopsy theater set up in the basement. Worn to a shadow of its former greatness, the Biltmore was then left, empty and abandoned, for two decades. While the golf course remained open, the spectacular hotel fell into disrepair at the mercy of nature, vandals, and time. The City of Coral Gables took over ownership of the 150-acre property, but there was little consensus on what to do with what was quickly becoming a large eyesore in the middle of a fading community of South Florida. They lopped the golf course in two—nine holes kept as a municipal track and nine holes turned into the private Riviera Country Club.

But while the Biltmore Hotel may have been left bereft of the living, Fatty and the spirits of hundreds of others who died there never moved out.

Late one night in 1979, Barbara Clipper, president of the local Science Fiction Club, led a group of members into the dark, spooky old hotel. They took along a tape recorder, hoping to capture some sort of supernatural activity. The group scoured the Biltmore but witnessed nothing. Or so they thought.

Dejected, the group went home and listened to the recordings. What they heard left them chilled. The tape very clearly captured about a minute's worth of tortured heavy breathing followed by a long sigh of resignation. Fatty Walsh's last moments captured on tape fifty years after his murder? Barbara doesn't know. But she is sure that the sounds on the tape were captured in what, to her group, appeared to be an empty, deathly silent old hotel. The breathing sounds could not have been made, she swears, by any members of her group or any animals.

It was around that time that locals, who had free run of the golf course in the evenings, began to report ghostly lights, crashing noises, and haunting music coming from the empty hotel. The ghost stories became so well known that on pleasant nights, hundreds would gather on the fairways to check out spooky lights and sounds coming from the decaying building. The spirits got so out of hand one night that Dade County sheriffs and Miami police raided the building, expecting to find vagrants and drug users inside. Eighteen cops and two search dogs scoured the place for hours. The Biltmore, however, was empty, at least of the living.

The hotel has made a miraculous comeback since the days of the Science Fiction Club rummaging through its abandoned halls and cops raiding its rotting interior. In 1983, the city of Coral Gables, which had taken ownership of the Biltmore property and the golf course, started a four-year, $55 million renovation effort to restore the place to its former grandeur. While the work returned luster to the Biltmore, it also sparked increased activity among the hotel's ghosts and goblins. The noises, apparitions, and unexplained happenings so unnerved the Cuban and Haitian workers that they demanded to be out of the place before dark.

Despite the continued spookiness, a gala reminiscent of the hotel's debut drew six hundred people to a black-tie New Year's Eve party to celebrate the Biltmore's reopening in 1987. The swimming pool was renovated in 1992. And in 2007, Brian Silva of Dover, New Hampshire, lovingly restored the Donald Ross course, rejoining the front and back nines into the original 6,742-yard, eighteen-hole layout.

And it has once again become a favorite South Florida getaway for the rich and powerful. Former President Bill Clinton is among the new Biltmore's regulars, having fallen in love with the hotel in 1994 when he hosted the Summit of the Americas there. Ever since, he's made the Biltmore a regular stop for both golf and R&R. But so haunted is the place that not even the ex-president can count on an incident-free stay.

Clinton, who prefers the suite frequented by Al Capone on the thirteenth floor, had settled in early one recent evening with plans to watch a football game on television. Inexplicably, the television could not be tuned to any station. The harder the former president tried, the more the device rebelled until finally it went into a fit of turning itself on and off at will. Secret Service agents failed to fix the possessed device and an exasperated President Clinton gave up and went to watch the game elsewhere.

What Bill Clinton encountered is but a small taste, however, of what employees and guests have experienced at the hands of Fatty's ghost and other Biltmore spirits for decades. As was his style, Fatty continues to lavish attention on the ladies, opening doors for waitresses carrying full trays and writing love notes on steamed-up mirrors. He's been known to steal lampshades and has a penchant for manipulating the elevators to trick guests, mostly attractive blond women, into riding to the thirteenth floor.

In one account, a couple trying to get to their fourth-floor room were taken to the thirteenth floor, where the doors opened on the suite where Fatty breathed his last. The doors stayed open and the elevator seemed stuck. When the wife, a statuesque blonde, stepped out of the lift to investigate, the doors slammed shut behind her and the helpless husband was whisked back down to the lobby.

She was left alone in the dark, empty suite. This was where Fatty once entertained powerful men and beautiful women in a nightly extravaganza of gambling, drinking, and song. It's also the place where he was shot dead just a few feet from where she now stood. Frozen in fear against the elevator doors, the woman heard someone moving around the room, dropping things on the floor and laughing quietly. The room turned ice cold, and she distinctly smelled cigar smoke. By the time her husband came to her rescue with the aid of hotel employees, the woman was sufficiently spooked to insist on leaving the hotel.

Fatty isn't alone in haunting a place with such a long, rich history, of course. Stories abound about the woman in white, a ghost who appears to guests and hotel staff as a real person, albeit very pale. Persistent tales that she may be a young mother who fell to her death from a balcony in the 1940s while trying to rescue her child seem unlikely. No record exists of such an accident, and the balcony railings in place at the time would have been difficult to climb over. That said, enough people have seen the apparition—usually on the ground floor, sometimes on the thirteenth floor— that the woman in white has become part of the Biltmore lore. Staff members say she always appears lost and sad. Many have mistaken her for a real guest and asked if she needs help, but she never responds. She simply disappears. She also has a knack for appearing in areas that are either locked or inaccessible to guests.

Even the woman in white is not alone. Psychics and para- normalists who have visited the Biltmore say it is one of the most haunted places in Florida. Hundreds of spirits—from old soldiers to jilted lovers to the ghosts of those whose bod- ies were stored in the medical school coolers—wander the halls in various states of restlessness.

Yes, there are hundreds of ghosts there, but the Biltmore is still, as ever, largely Fatty's place.

Area historian and storyteller Kathi Gathercole spent years studying the Biltmore's history and its ghost stories as part of her job. She knows all of the Fatty Walsh legends by heart and has talked to countless hotel employees who swear they've witnessed Fatty's spirit in action. Still, she never really believed any of the tales about the mobster ghost.

Until last year.

Kathi was doing a storytelling session for a group of young people. Two of the kids in the group were accompanied by a nanny, a stunning young blonde. When the class broke up, the young woman and her charges made their way to the elevators, where they found the machines flashing and generally misbehaving. After pushing several buttons, the nanny boarded the lift, only to have the doors slam shut, separating her from the children. She was taken to the thirteenth floor, where the elevator opened and refused to budge. The frightened young woman ventured out and found the thirteenth-floor suite unlocked, even though it was vacant. She called the concierge, who sent hotel staff to rescue her.

"This happened right in front of me," says Kathi, who had heard for years about Fatty's insatiable taste for pretty blondes. "Yet, I still didn't believe it."

Kathi decided to try an experiment—with her own daughter as bait.

Elizabeth Gathercole is twenty-five years old, blond, and as appealing as any young socialite who ever caught Fatty's eye. Her mother, Kathi, figured she'd make the perfect lure for the wiseguy's ghost. Sure enough, as soon as Elizabeth got near the elevators, the lights began to flash and the elevator arrived on their floor without being called.

Elizabeth and her sister-in-law stepped into the car. Nothing happened. The lift sat there, lifeless. Fatty wanted the pretty blonde. Alone.

The women got out, then, nervously, Elizabeth stepped back inside. Without her pressing a single button, the doors closed and the elevator started going up.

"It did exactly what everyone said it would do," Kathi says. "It took her up to the thirteenth floor. It opened. And it stuck there."

Elizabeth was trapped for a while on the thirteenth floor, where she too found the empty suite, which is always kept locked, wide open. The concierge seemed rather bored when he came to retrieve the woman from Fatty's favorite haunt. "It's no big deal," he said. "I do this a couple of times a week. Whenever I see a pretty blonde near the elevators, I get my keys out and get ready to go up to the thirteenth floor."

Chapter 7

Henry Longhurst: A Message from the Other Side

For all his sensational golf reporting during his illustrious career,
Golf Digest *scribe Henry Longhurst's greatest scoop may have*
come after he died.

Henry Longhurst was not merely a great golf writer; he was a great writer, period. For forty years he covered the game for the *Sunday Times* of London, the first golf correspondent in the storied newspaper's history. For many years, Longhurst also wrote for the American-based magazine *Golf Digest*.

His deft use of the language, along with his keen observations and knack for unearthing telling details made his stories about the world's greatest golfers and the world's finest courses come alive for millions of readers every week. Witness his description of Arnold Palmer at the 1961 Open at Royal Birkdale for the *Sunday Times:*

"It is doubtful that there was a man present at Birkdale who wanted Palmer to lose. It's impossible to over-praise the tact and charm with which this American has conducted himself on his two visits to Britain. He has no fancy airs or graces; he wears no fancy clothes; he makes no fancy speeches. He simply says and does exactly the right thing at the right time, and that is enough."

Longhurst became well known for amassing a mountain of humorous quotes about the game, including: "Playing golf is like learning a foreign language," "They say 'practice makes perfect.' Of course, it doesn't. For the vast majority of golfers it merely consolidates imperfection," and "Golfing excellence goes hand and hand with alcohol, as many an Open and Amateur champion has shown."

After leaving the *Sunday Times,* he became a golf commentator for the BBC in Great Britain. American golf fans grew familiar with Longhurst's learned style when he served, remarkably, as a color commentator for both CBS and ABC television at the same time. Through his analysis of the sport during tournament coverage, Americans came to fall in love with televised golf. The words Longhurst used to describe the action simultaneously educated and entertained the viewers. Audiences worldwide sat in rapt attention as Longhurst painted his word pictures during such memorable broadcasts as the Open Championships held on the great courses of the United Kingdom.

In addition to being a talented wordsmith, Longhurst was also an excellent golfer. He was captain of his golf team at Cambridge University and later won the German amateur title. Longhurst also dabbled in politics, serving two years as a member of Parliament. He was never reelected.

But for all the enrapturing words he spoke and all the eloquent phrases he penned, Longhurst's greatest reporting just might have come after he died. It took decades for the story of Longhurst's final report to come to light, and it involved a man who had been a dear friend to him through the last years of his life.

English World War II hero Sir Douglas Bader's story sounds like a far-fetched myth but is, in fact, all true.

Bader was born in London in 1910, the second son of Major Frederick Roberts Bader of Britain's Royal Engineers and his wife, Jessie. His older brother, Frederick, fought and died in France during World War I, while his father died in a hospital in Saint-Omer. An athletic lad, the young Bader played both cricket and football in school. He also received special tutoring as a result of having lost his father in the war. The combination of his physical prowess and the guidance he received from his teachers landed Bader a spot as a cadet training to fly for the Royal Air Force.

On December 14, 1931, shortly after earning his wings in the RAF, Bader visited Reading Aero Club. He began showing off his aerobatic skills on a dare in a Bristol Bulldog, an aircraft with which he was unfamiliar. He was performing one of his favorite maneuvers, taking the plane through a number of slow rolls at low altitude. RAF regulations prohibited such moves at an altitude of less than one thousand feet. Bader was doing the rolls just thirty feet above Woodley airfield when suddenly his left wing tip clipped the ground, sending him into a spin. As a result of the crash, Bader, then just twenty years old, underwent a double amputation—losing one leg below the knee and the other just above the knee. He made a brief, cryptic mention of the incident in his pilot's logbook for that day.

"Crashed slow-rolling near ground," he wrote with faltering hand. "Bad show."

Bader petitioned to remain in the RAF, but his request was denied. Despite his formidable skills as a pilot, he was dismissed from military service and forced to return to civilian life. He married his sweetheart, Thelma, a short time later.

It was about this time, at the age of twenty-five, that Bader took up golf. His first attempt at the sport was hardly encouraging. Bader grabbed a seven-iron and steadied himself on his artificial legs. He dropped a ball on the grass and took a mighty swing at it. He missed the ball by a foot and spun himself around so violently, he landed on his back. Oddly, the spill seemed to fuel Bader's desire. He repeated the effort over and over and over again, missing the ball and landing flat on his back each time. On the twelfth try, he fell again but did manage to top the ball weakly. The contact boosted his confidence. A series of misses and falls followed, then on the twenty-fifth try he topped the ball weakly once again and crashed into the turf.

"I think you've had enough for today," Thelma said to him, trying to lure him from the frustrating and increasingly dangerous pursuit. He gave up for the evening but was back at it the next day. He learned to balance himself better, slowing his backswing and shortening his swing. He knocked the ball about thirty yards on the fly. Now he was hooked. Within a week he could hit the ball solidly and remain standing nine out of ten times.

It was no easy feat. His prosthetics chafed his skin bloody and raw as he tromped over the uneven ground of his local golf course at North Hants. Early into any round, Bader would be drenched in sweat from the effort required to swing with his upper body, then travel from shot to shot and hole to hole. It took months before he could tolerate stringing together even three or four holes.

Bader could manage only about 150 yards per shot, but the balance he'd learned from trying to stay standing after each shot kept the bulk of his shots straight and true. He excelled in areas where other players held less of a physical advantage over him; he avoided trouble and developed a terrific short game. Keeping the ball in play started to result in more pars and the occasional birdie. As his game improved, his confidence grew. Thelma agreed to caddy for him.

About a year after taking up the game, Bader completed a full eighteen holes for the first time. By all accounts, the poor guy was so exhausted, his playing partners politely stopped counting his quickly mounting score near the end. Bader was thrilled by the experience.

"I feel so fresh I could do another nine," he told his wife after the round.

"No, you don't!" she snapped back.

A month after that first full round, Bader broke 100 for the first time. A month after that, he played thirty-six holes in one day.

But his best golf days were still years away.

When World War II broke out, Bader saw an opportunity to get off the golf course and back into the air. He applied for reinstatement to the RAF, and the British government, desperate for qualified airmen to sustain the growing war effort, quickly granted his request. He ended up commanding a Canadian group of fliers that had suffered heavy losses against the Germans before he arrived. Bader's enthusiasm and experience injected life back into the unit, and within a short time they were considered one of the best flying units in the Allied force. Known as equal parts motivator and bully, he quickly became an enigmatic figure among wartime aviators.

Asked to describe Bader, a fellow pilot once remarked: "He was not a particularly pleasant man, by turns arrogant, obstreperous and egotistical, but he made use of those qualities to do things which lesser men didn't have a hope of doing. He was certainly not an angel, but he was remarkable."

Remarkable indeed, and Bader had an odd advantage over his able-bodied aviation counterparts. The high G forces that caused other pilots to black out when blood rushed to their extremities never affected Bader. As a result, he flew like a demon possessed. Using his two metal prostheses for legs, Bader wracked up twenty-two confirmed kills, putting him among the top five fighter aces in the RAF. But his success as a fighter pilot was short-lived. Something went horribly wrong in the skies over France on August 9, 1941. According to Bader's accounts, his Spitfire had been clipped in the tail by a German Messerschmitt 109. Subsequent inquiry indicates Bader may have actually been brought down by friendly fire after he got separated from his squadron. Regardless of the cause, Bader was once again saved by his lack of real legs. As the plane went down, one of his metal feet became trapped in a mangled rudder pedal. Had he not been able to disconnect his fake leg from his body, he would not have been able to bail out. Bader left his artificial limbs in the cockpit and hit the silk.

Bader parachuted to earth, sans legs, landing on a farm in Le Touquet in the northern part of France. A local farmer and a nurse hid the legless pilot for several days in a nearby barn, but he was eventually captured by the Germans in Saint-Omer, within sight of where his father had died. In a remarkable set of occurrences and through a series of negotiations, a decorated German fighter pilot who met Bader while he was a prisoner of war worked it out so that a British plane was allowed to drop a new set of artificial legs to Bader. Although it was a humanitarian gesture on the part of the Nazis, it would be one they would come to regret. Bader set about making it his business to escape the Nazi prison camps using his new German-made legs. On one occasion in particular, it was discovered Bader was missing only when a German ace came to visit him and found the British prisoner's bunk stuffed with rolled blankets and straw.

His repeated escape attempts landed Bader in the worst fix of his young life. He was transferred to Germany's infamous and virtually escape-proof Colditz Castle in Dresden. There he waited out the rest of the war.

Once the war was over, Bader was released and sent home, where he received a promotion to captain. In a spectacular heroes' homecoming, Bader piloted the lead plane in a three-hundred–aircraft victory flyover in London. He retired from the military in 1946 and went to work for Shell Aircraft, retiring from his civilian job in 1970.

Meanwhile, by the late 1970s, Longhurst was in his seventies and dying of cancer. His home was the famed Clayton Windmills, known locally as the Jack and Jill windmills, on the South Downs in West Sussex, England. The matching windmills were built in 1821, and in addition to grinding corn, the buildings afforded a stunning view of Sussex Weald. For a while, Longhurst lived in the two-story Jack windmill but later moved into another house on the property built in 1963. One of his frequent visitors over the last years of his life was Bader, who in addition to golf also shared Longhurst's love of gin.

By this time, Bader had fully rekindled the passion for golf he'd developed before the war. He and Longhurst, himself a scratch golfer, had hit it off on the course and were now regular playing partners. Longhurst's friendship and keen observation helped Bader immensely. For example, Longhurst noticed that his friend always hit perfect approach shots to the green on the 5th hole at North Hants. The reason, the journalist surmised, was the gentle upslope of the fairway.

"You should cut a half inch off your right leg," Longhurst told Bader. "Then you'll always be playing with an uphill lie."

What started as a joke soon became reality for the war veteran. Despite being warned by doctors the uneven prosthetics could cause irreparable spinal injury, Bader had his fake leg altered to gain the advantage.

"Wish I could do the same," the able-bodied Longhurst said, only half joking.

The trick worked as Bader shot under 80 for the first time a short time later. He lowered his handicap to an impressive four. Several years later, he had the lengths of his prosthetics corrected when he discovered he no longer needed the advantage of the faux uphill address.

By most accounts, Bader was an insufferable braggart about his golf game. But in a strange way, he found the irritation and annoyance he engendered in his fellow golfers a comfort. In the clubhouse, while bending some poor bloke's ear about his exploits on the links, Douglas Bader was just one of the guys, not some disabled fellow requiring special treatment.

It was that regular-guy Bader who greatly enjoyed engaging Longhurst in deep, late-night conversations where the pair could try to solve the problems of golf and politics and life. The night would end only when the gin bottle was empty.

On one such evening the conversation turned, as it often does among men getting on in years, to the subject of what truly lay beyond this mortal plane. It's one of life's great mysteries, after all. These two, Bader and Longhurst, managed to boil the matter down to a simple question: Will the grass be greener on the other side?

Understandably, it was a relevant topic for a man such as Longhurst so close to death. It was equally important to Bader, who had stared death in the face many times in his youth and cheated the grim reaper not just a few times. They were not religious men, but the subject captivated them on this particular evening. Neither took any firm side in the matter, though it would seem Longhurst held more firmly to the thought that there was something better awaiting us on the other side. The grass was greener there, he believed. They discussed it at length until the wee hours, when daylight and a lack of gin extinguished the debate.

Not long after, on the night of July 21, 1978, cancer won its final round against Henry Longhurst. He was dead. One of the great voices in golf had been silenced, so it seemed. Mourning his good friend, Bader forgot about the deep, spiritual conversation they'd had.

Enter English golf writer Peter Dobereiner, who recounted the legendary story of what ensued to his good friend Jerry Tarde, the editor-in-chief of *Golf Digest,* who wrote a column about it in 2000.

As Dobereiner told it, a few months after Longhurst died, Bader was in London to speak at a dinner. As he stepped from his cab, he saw a woman standing by the side of the street. She was disheveled and unkempt. She appeared to be homeless, perhaps a beggar. As soon as Bader spied her, the woman made eye contact and headed directly for him. The old war veteran recoiled as she approached.

"Are you Sir Douglas Bader?" the woman asked.

"Yes. Yes, I am," Bader replied. "Who are you?"

"I'm a clairvoyant," she replied. "I have a message from a friend of yours."

"Who? What friend?" Bader asked.

"I know him only as Henry," the woman answered.

Bader was stunned at the mention of his old friend's name.

"And what is the message?" Bader asked with a mix of curiosity and dread. He could not have been prepared for her answer.

"He said, 'Tell Bader: The grass is greener on the other side.'"

Bader, shaken by the encounter, jumped back into the cab in which he'd come, immediately returning home and skipping the dinner appearance altogether. Bader never mentioned the fantastic encounter to anyone other than Dobereiner for the rest of his days.

These days, skeptics like to point out that Longhurst was a man of great wit and humor. It isn't far-fetched at all to consider that he staged the entire thing as an elaborate practical joke on his old friend Douglas Bader. With the question of their mortality still hanging and Longhurst's own death looming, it would have been perfectly in keeping with his character to pay an old woman to act the part of a shabby street psychic. He might well have put her up to finding the old pilot and accosting him with a tale of voices from beyond the grave.

Most who have heard the tale think that's unlikely, however. Certainly Bader believed the message came from Henry from somewhere in the great beyond. Longhurst, ever the journalist, felt compelled to report what he'd seen and could only tell the truth of what he found there.

Dobereiner, forever a part of the Longhurst story when it is retold, was himself a remarkable man, who before covering golf was a writer for the groundbreaking BBC television satire *That Was the Week that Was.*

Fellow golf writer Dai Davies, who replaced Dobereiner at both the *Guardian* and *Observer,* said of him, "He was, perhaps, the most rounded man, the most civilized man, even the most erudite man to embrace and grace a golfing press tent."

Jerry Tarde first met Dobereiner at the 1977 Walker Cup matches, held at Shinnecock Hills Golf Club on the southeastern tip of Long Island. They became great friends, as did their families.

"Peter was a very special man. He was the kind of guy who, for no good reason, would take you under his wing and be nice to you," Tarde says. "Peter was a remarkable writer, a terrible golfer, and he loved the game."

Although Dobereiner was considered the one who took up the position of golf writer for a generation after Longhurst retired, he did not view his role that way.

"Peter always felt he wasn't fit to carry the bag of Longhurst as a writer," Tarde said, disagreeing with his friend's self-assessment. "Longhurst was the better golfer, but there was no doubt who was the better writer."

This is an example of Dobereiner's wit and style from the 1983 Open Championship:

"At Birkdale, the players will encounter terrain and vegetation and golfing dilemmas such as they have never met before. All their powers of resourcefulness, stoicism, patience and survival will be examined to the limit—and that is just trying to get a cup of coffee through room service."

Or this assessment of his fellow countrymen:

"The British do not appreciate change, especially from the ladies. Golf has been soaking in male chauvinist piggery for 500 years and it can't be eradicated overnight."

Tarde says he can think of only one explanation as to why Dobereiner took so long to reveal the story: He was waiting for Bader, himself, to find whether the grass was greener.

Dobereiner, although reticent to speak in public, was a wonderful storyteller, and the version of the tale he told of Longhurst never changed in the few times he recounted it to Tarde.

Dobereiner, for his part, never revealed whether he believed that it was Longhurst sending a message from beyond the grave or whether his old friend was pulling off one of the greatest hoaxes of all time.

"It's one of those mysteries you believe or don't believe," Tarde says. "Write your own ending."

Perhaps Sir Douglas Bader, who was knighted by the queen in 1972, has already done that for himself.

On September 5, 1982, the seventy-two-year-old Bader was the featured speaker at the ninetieth birthday party of fellow aviator Sir Arthur "Bomber" Harris in London. After regaling the crowd with his tales of derring-do, Bader left the party. A short time later, he lay dead of a heart attack. Perhaps he has discovered the veracity of Longhurst's correspondence from beyond the grave. Only now does he know for sure whether the grass really is greener in the great beyond.

Chapter 8

Ahwahnee and Wawona Hotels: The Rustic Ghosts of Yosemite

A trip to the pair of famous lodges in Yosemite National Park can provide the visitor with breathtaking scenery, a unique golf experience, and perhaps an encounter with ghosts, including one that many think is the spirit of the thirty-fifth president of the United States.

The Ahwahnee and Wawona hotels, both National Historic Landmarks, have been welcoming visitors to Yosemite National Park in their own distinctive style for decades.

Since 1927 the Ahwahnee has stood majestically on the site of what was once a Miwok Indian village in the northeast end of Yosemite Valley. Designed from the outset to attract the upper classes to the park, the remote locale for this exclusive sanctuary was selected because of its exposure to the sun, as well as for the breathtaking views it affords of Yosemite's most famous attractions, including Half Dome, Yosemite Falls, and Glacier Point. With rooms that approach $1,000 a night, this six-story rock and iron hotel today remains a popular destination for the affluent looking to take in the beauty of Yosemite while also enjoying first-class accommodations and gourmet fare.

Architect Gilbert Stanley Underwood was commissioned in 1925 to design the elite hotel. He was assisted by art historians Dr. Phyllis Ackerman and Professor Arthur Upham Pope, who were hired to oversee the interior tile, wood, metal, and plaster work. The result is a decor that elegantly combines a variety of distinct styles, including Art Deco, Native American, Middle Eastern, and Arts and Crafts. It was Ackerman and Pope who brought in the now-famous kilim and soumak rugs scattered throughout the common areas of the 150,000-foot hotel.

While the lodge is designed to appear as if wood plays a major role in the structure, it actually does not. Concrete dyed to resemble redwoods—yet resist fire—has fooled guests since the hotel opened. Over one thousand tons of steel and five thousand tons of building stone were brought to the secluded location. The creation now has twenty-four-foot-high ceilings, a 6,300-square-foot dining room with ninety-nine guest rooms and twenty-four bungalows near the Merced River.

Famed Yosemite photographer and former Ahwahnee employee Ansel Adams adored the hotel, as displayed in his writing of the place: "Yet on entering The Ahwahnee one is conscious of calm and complete beauty echoing the mood of majesty and peace that is the essential quality of Yosemite. . . . Against a background of forest and precipice the architect has nestled the great structure of granite, scaling his design with sky and space and stone. To the interior all ornamentation has been confined, and therein lies a miracle of color and design. The Indian motif is supreme. The designs are stylized with tasteful sophistication; decidedly Indian, yet decidedly more than Indian, they epitomize the involved and intricate symbolism of primitive man."

It was Adams who inaugurated the Bracebridge Dinner, a four-hour, seven-course extravaganza hosted around Christmastime in the Ahwahnee's grand dining hall that is made up to look like a seventeenth-century English manor. The presentation is based on an amalgamation of Washington Irving stories and has occurred every year since 1927 (except during World War II, when the Ahwahnee was transformed into a naval hospital for convalescing wounded soldiers). Adams served as director as well as an actor in the evening's entertainment.

Whether or not they took part in the Bracebridge Dinner, a litany of the famous has signed the guest book, including Brad Pitt, Lucille Ball (while filming *The Long, Long Trailer*), Judy Garland, Mel Gibson (while filming *Maverick*), Charlton Heston, Douglas Fairbanks Jr., Joan Baez, Boris Karloff, and Kim Novak. In addition to these well-known names and faces, a number of the nation's top political leaders found lodging at the place: John F. Kennedy stayed at the Ahwahnee, as did Herbert Hoover and Eleanor Roosevelt. The grand structure has also been host to Queen Ratana of Nepal, King Baudouin of Belgium, Ethiopian Emperor Haile Selassie, and, in 1983, Queen Elizabeth and Prince Philip.

As one might imagine, with all these comings and goings there are bound to be visitors who stay beyond their welcome. There have been reports of something—or someone—roaming the sixth floor of the grand hotel for the past three decades, and many believe it is the ghost of Mary Curry Tresidder, who with her husband, Donald, was instrumental in the hotel's early success. Her parents owned the Yosemite Park and Curry Company, a popular park concession. Mary also authored the book *The Trees of Yosemite*. Her husband earned his medical degree from Stanford University, eventually becoming president of his wife's family's company, as well as of Stanford.

Donald died of a heart attack in 1948, while Mary lived twenty-two more years, passing away just two days before Halloween in 1970. Her apartment was converted into the Tresidder Suite, and it was not long after her death that the sightings began in and around her former living quarters. Employees and guests have seen Mary moving silently through the old hotel as if still on some important mission there.

Mary's is not the only spirit in the grand structure. For years, in the parlor on the third floor, staff have reported seeing a rocking chair, even though the hotel has never had one. The reports of the apparition are almost always the same: Someone sees the chair and hurries to tell coworkers about the experience. When others looking to corroborate the story get to the spot where the chair was seen, they always find it has vanished.

According to former employee Jack Hicks, there was only one occasion when a rocking chair was brought into the hotel and that was for President John F. Kennedy during his 1962 visit to Yosemite. Hicks, who was maître d' at the time, says Kennedy also brought along his own switchboard and that, like the rocking chair, was removed when Kennedy departed. Could it be the ghost of JFK returning to the Ahwahnee for a leisurely rock?

The Wawona Hotel, just a few miles away, is the polar opposite of the Ahwahnee. At the Wawona, visitors step directly back into 1879, leaving behind many modern conveniences. The centerpiece of this retreat is the large white wooden hotel with its distinctive green room and large wraparound porch. There are no in-room telephones or televisions, and only a few rooms in the hotel or in the free-standing cabins surrounding it have their own bathrooms. Instead there are common ones—unheated—on each floor of the hotel. In the first-floor parlor, historian and pianist Tom Bopp entertains the guests with tales of Yosemite and sing-alongs with tunes from throughout the hotel's life span.

Room rates are under $190.

Lest you think the Wawona too base to attract the rich and powerful, rest assured the place has hosted its share of high rollers who shunned the Ahwahnee's luxuries for a taste of the Wawona's rustic charms. The most famous guest of the Wawona was Ulysses S. Grant, who in 1879, two years after he left the White House, vacationed there. Grant was then recently back from an around-the-world trip with his wife, Julia, and son Frederick. He had visited every country in Europe in addition to others, including Japan, China, Burma, and Siam (now Thailand).

He was greeted by an enthusiastic crowd upon his return to San Francisco in September 1879, later telling a group of Confederate veterans, "I have an abiding faith that we will remain together in future harmony."

It was from there that he and his family headed to Yosemite and the Wawona Hotel. One can picture Grant, whom Mark Twain described as having "iron serenity," stoically sitting on the porch awash in the glory of Yosemite Valley.

The precursor to the hotel was a result of the California Gold Rush. Worn out by the rigors of mining, Galen Clark established Clark Station in 1857. The small wooden structure, which sat very near the present-day hotel, was established to feed miners making their way to and from the digs.

Called "palahchun" by the local Indians, meaning "a good place to stop," the location is four thousand feet above sea level and halfway between the foothills and Yosemite Valley. Six miles away is the famous Mariposa Grove of sequoias.

Clark may very well have been a wonderful host and cook, but he was not a successful businessman. In fact, he nearly lost the enterprise altogether before selling what by then was known as Big Tree Station to Henry Washburn, who was soon joined by his three brothers to help in the growing endeavor. It was Henry's wife, Jean, who, upon completion of the hotel in 1879, suggested the name be changed to Wawona, the word for "big tree" in the language of the North Fork Mono tribe.

Though the Ahwahnee has the amenities, the Wawona does trump its neighbor in one area: golf. Where the Ahwahnee once had a small course for its clientele that over the years has included royalty and the Hollywood elite, the Wawona still possesses a delightful nine-hole layout that begins and ends in a meadow across the street from the hotel. A quaint throwback pro shop is still housed at one end of the ground floor. The Wawona Golf Course, one of only two inside a United States national park, has remained in its current incarnation for decades and cannot be altered in the slightest without a serious review process by the National Park Service.

It was Henry's nephew Clarence Washburn in the second decade of the 1900s who introduced outdoor activities to the Wawona as a way to entice visitors. He built a swimming tank and a croquet court and would soon be responsible for the golf course. The Walter G. Fovargue design was an instant success. As a result of his involvement, Clarence even took up the game and appeared to have become enamored with it. In his diary he noted the birth of his child with the words "baby born," while Fovargue's efforts received more attention: "Mr. Fovargue laying out golf course in meadow," he wrote.

Though the course at the Ahwahnee is gone, lodgers there are allowed to make the short drive to the Wawona and tee up at the par-35 course. Of course, the hotels share something else aside from a golf course—ghost stories.

Kim Porter, now the golf course superintendent, has worked on the course since 1980 but has been in the valley since 1974. In his early days, he recalls, he heard reports of people seeing what came to be known as the Viking. Some said it was a ghost, possibly of a gold miner, seen wandering around the course. Others said it was a real mountain man, who escaped the encroaching society by retreating back into the dense forest. There were even stories that he would come out at night and take care of the course, perhaps hand watering a green or two.

The Viking's appearance, however, was not always welcomed, according to Porter.

"At dusk or at night there'd be a couple out walking on the course admiring the views or looking at the stars and he'd come out of the woods and scare them," Porter says. And in this remote place, the Viking is not alone.

There's also the ghost pilot seen on the stairs of Moore Cottage, one of the Wawona's guest cabins.

What is now Wawona Meadow, adjacent to the second hole of the golf course, was once a landing strip for visitors who had their own airplanes. During the 1920s, one of those planes missed its approach badly and crashed, seriously injuring the pilot, who was taken to Moore Cottage to await medical attention. Sadly, the man died before a doctor arrived. Ever since, guests and staff have reported seeing the ghost clad in a leather jacket and leather flying helmet, complete with goggles and white scarf, walking the inside stairs of Moore Cottage.

The Wawona is also the scene of one other oft-repeated incident witnessed by employees in 1985. At the time, the hotel's workers were housed on the second floor of the hotel and Room 220 was used as a sort of employee lounge. One night, a group of staff members was watching television when, according to one witness's account, a ten-foot area rug rose up and levitated perhaps three inches off the floor. As the workers watched in awe, the carpet floated to the other side of the room. Most of the staffers beat a hasty retreat out of the room, but those brave enough to stay say they saw something quite amazing and unexplained. The carpet continued to float around the room, then effortlessly drifted back to where it started. Without a sound, the rug descended to its original position on the floor. It has never moved on its own since.

Chapter 9

Stafford Country Club: Dare to Sleep with Demons

For most, the chance to not only visit, but to spend the night—a long, dark night—in the blood-stained room where a horrific murder took place is not on the to-do list. In fact, it might top the not-to-do list. But for one brave teen, staring down the ghosts of Stafford Country Club was a test of his budding manhood.

Few would revel in the opportunity to meet fear and death face to face. At eighteen years old and fresh out of high school, Max Mason was one of those rare people who did. His ludicrous endeavor did not, however, take place in some foreboding castle high in the mountains of Transylvania or at an abandoned Victorian mansion at the end of some dark, deserted road. It happened in 1936 at the private Stafford Country Club amid the rolling farmland of upstate New York, just outside of Rochester.

The events that led him and his best friend to that haunted place began more than a decade earlier.

It was in the early 1920s when a cadre of businessmen from the New York towns of Batavia and Leroy came together with the idea of building a top-notch country club for Genesee County. By the end of 1921 their vision was coming to fruition with the completion of the first nine holes of the golf course. Walter Travis designed the layout to be built over farmland on the banks of Black Creek in the township of Stafford.

In October of that year, the great golfer Walter Hagen, a native of Rochester, New York, visited the site and raved about what he saw. The dapper and controversial Hagen was on his way to becoming one of the preeminent golfers of the day. Earlier in 1921 he'd captured his second Western Open, then considered an important tournament, and the first of his five PGA Championships to go along with the two U.S. Opens he already had under his belt.

He said of Stafford, to the delight of the founders, "second to none and worthy of the interest of its members for years to come."

Within six years, however, the course would be attracting interest in ways no one could have imagined. On a still August morning in 1927, one employee murdered another in a grisly scene of brutality that stains Stafford Country Club to this day. The killer was Charles Ball, a well-built man of twenty-six who was in charge of the club's locker room. He was a liked and trusted employee who had come to Stafford in April of that year. The victim was club steward Charles Knoblock, sixty-two, a slight man in his third season at Stafford, married with two children.

Knoblock and Ball shared quarters on the second floor of the clubhouse above the kitchen, the only employees who resided on the grounds during the golfing season. By all accounts they got along well.

What really happened on the morning of August 18, 1927, is unknown. The previous afternoon Ball had told employees he was going to a dance in nearby Leroy. It is assumed he returned to the club later that evening. At around 4:15 a.m. on the day of the murder, someone from inside the club attempted to make a collect long-distance call, never volunteering his identity to the operator assisting him. The man hung up abruptly when she informed him she needed his name to make the connection.

Within a few hours the attack would take place, apparently unprovoked.

The murder was recounted in ghoulish detail by the *Batavia Daily News* under the headline: NEGRO WITH CLUB BUTCHER KNIFE MURDERED A PORTER AT STAFFORD. The paper called the confrontation a "ghastly struggle," with few, if any, images left to the imagination.

Samuel Boldt went to the club early every morning to get table scraps for chicken feed. On that August morning, Boldt was surprised to find neither Knoblock nor Ball in the kitchen eating breakfast as they normally did. He called out for the two men and heard only a feeble moaning in response. Realizing Knoblock was beckoning him, Boldt went upstairs, where he "made his terrifying discovery."

According to the newspaper accounts, "Boldt was unnerved by the terrible sight of Knoblock lying on the blood-soaked bed, with the floor almost completely coated and the walls spattered with red, the furnishings broken and the clothing scattered about."

As he lay bleeding to death, Knoblock with gasping breaths was able to partially recount what happened. He told Boldt he had awakened to a crazed Ball standing over his bed, butcher knife in hand, demanding he get up and make breakfast, which he did every morning. Knoblock said that as he rose to defend himself, Ball began slashing, stopping the assault as quickly as he started it, and then fleeing the building.

Boldt ran half a mile to the nearest house to summon help. What the police found when they arrived was reported in detail by the Batavia newspaper.

"Knoblock had on only a shirt. His entire body was covered with blood oozing from a dozen or more knife slashes. The most serious one was on the left side of his head extending from the scalp through the ear, down the side of his neck and across the throat but not into the jugular vein. Another severe one extended from above the left wrist across the hand and fingers nearly severing some of the fingers. There was another deep slash on his left arm through the elbow, exposing the bones. There were many other smaller slashes on various parts of the body."

Knoblock died later that morning at the hospital after giving Boldt a more complete account of the attack. Detectives pieced the victim's story together with clues at the scene to develop a more detailed account of the killer's movements once he ceased slashing his mortally wounded coworker.

The cops said Ball wore a pair of golf shoes with small circles on the rubber soles. Bloody footprints with those unique markings were found leading from Knoblock's bed into Ball's own sleeping quarters and from there down to the stairway, through the kitchen and to the cigar stand in another part of the club. The killer evidently helped himself hurriedly to cigarettes and cigars before he fled.

Local and state police converged on the scene looking for the killer, but it was a young club employee who made the most important discovery. That morning, caddy John Davis stumbled upon the murder weapon. The eighteen-inch knife with a wooden handle had been tossed into the bushes down an embankment behind the caddy house.

"It had a razor-like edge, and the authorities found a sharpening stone on the kitchen table where Ball had apparently put an edge on it before making his attack," read the account.

The knife may have been located, but Ball was nowhere to be found. For four days, the state police conducted the most intense manhunt in county history.

Desperate and on the lam, Ball turned up looking for food at a farm where he had worked. At about 8 p.m., as the sun was setting, W. G. Coverdale heard a knock on the woodshed door and answered, finding before him the man wanted for murder.

"Do you know who I am?" Ball asked.

"Yes," Coverdale responded, unafraid of the murderer. "You are Chester Ball."

"I've been on the bum for about a week," Ball answered. "Will you give me something to eat?"

Coverdale told police that he gave Ball four slices of bread and when he asked for water, Coverdale pointed to the nearby pump. It was the last he saw of Ball.

Finally, a tip from Ernest Hutchinson, a boy in the neighboring town of Leroy who received a $1,000 reward for his information, led to the capture of Ball. Four days after the killing, police had their man.

"Weakened by hunger, [Ball] was staggering through the fields on the outskirts of the village of Leroy when he was seen by two troopers patrolling the road in an automobile," read the newspaper story. Troopers William Cannon and G. W. Donnelly made the arrest.

"Ball walked into their hands and made no resistance when accosted. He was loaded into the car and started on the trip for the barracks but was in such a weakened condition that the troopers made a stop at a Leroy restaurant where Ball eagerly gulped down a half gallon of coffee."

Ball was convicted on a count of second-degree murder and sentenced to no less than twenty years in prison.

A little more than eight years after the crime, Max Mason and one of his good buddies made the decision to sleep in the room where the murder had taken place.

"There was two or three of us that had graduated from high school—this was way back in '35—we played golf and when we came back—we weren't old enough yet—we had a couple of beers and some dinner," says Mason, now ninety years old. In an eerie coincidence, his birthday, August 22, is also the date of Ball's capture.

The manager of the club suggested the teens spend the night upstairs, a challenge, no doubt, of their manhood. One of the friends passed on the invitation to sleep in the room, but another, Herb Kriske, a bartender at the club and high school classmate of Mason's, accepted the offer. Mason, whose family were club members at Stafford, joined in on the dare.

"It was spur of the moment," says Mason of the decision.

Mason was not just another son of a member; his father, Max Sr., and his uncle, Roy Mason, were founding members of the club. Max Jr. had been caddying at the Stafford for several years prior to accepting the spooky challenge to bunk for the night at the scene of the grisly murder.

Well aware of the awful details of the crime, the two brave teens climbed the stairs—the same ones Ernest Ball hurried down as he fled the scene—and found themselves in the two adjoining rooms, the ones Ball and Knoblock shared. If the two teenagers assumed any and all remnants of the crime had long ago dissipated, they were wrong; they were shocked to find the walls were still covered with Knoblock's dried blood.

"The fear wasn't there until we saw the bloodstains," Mason says.

Still, he and Kriske decided to spend the night using the two beds that were still in the rooms. Accompanying them was an unseen presence that Mason claims remained for the entire night.

"It gave us a real uneasy feeling," he says.

Mason still laughs at the recollection of their evening, which he said passed without incident. But neither those two, nor anyone else to his knowledge, ever again spent a night in those rooms. Some years afterward they were converted into a storage area.

Mason became an individual member of the club in 1939, the same year he married Jane. The couple have since made quite a bit of history of their own at Stafford. The two were extremely successful golfers, even holding the record for the most Mr. and Mrs. Scratch Championships. Max was club president in 1961 and has served on many boards since then. He and Jane continue to maintain the many bluebird houses around the club property.

During all those years, the memory of the most brutal day in Stafford's history would be conjured one more time, sometime in the 1960s, if Mason remembers correctly.

"I was up in the clubhouse and a man was sitting there in a chair having a cup of coffee," Mason says. He asked an employee who it was, and the answer stunned him: Chester Ball.

Ball had apparently been released from prison a short time before and came to visit the club. He stayed perhaps an hour talking with a few employees, Mason says, then left, never to be seen at Stafford Country Club again.

Chapter 10
St. Andrews: A Rich and Bloody History

For golfers, St. Andrews is a combination of the Garden of Eden, heaven, Mecca, the Holy Grail, and perfection incarnate, all located on the east coast of Scotland. But the rugged beauty of golf's birthplace masks a bloody history that has left nearly every berm, hedgerow, and cobblestone stained with some tale of the macabre.

The towheaded young Scot held his head up in a sort of gentle defiance, listening to the charges against him.

"You, sir, are a heretic!" the Dominican Friar Campbell shouted. The archbishop of St. Andrews and his panel of bishops, abbots, and other clergy nodded and murmured in agreement.

"No, sir, I am no heretic," Patrick Hamilton replied, shifting forward in the dock where he stood with a dozen other accused religious reformers. He had a calm intensity well beyond his twenty-four years. "And I do not believe you really judge me so, brother."

The prisoners had been dragged at first light up Pends Road to the priory to hear church officials call them devils and demand their executions. Hamilton, himself a grandson of King James II and an ordained priest, scanned the panel of judges. His accusers included a thirteen-year-old boy and a monk named Patrick Hepburn well known for his eleven illegitimate children and his insatiable appetite for prostitutes.

"Hepburn takes special pleasure in burning those who seek comfort in God's word," Hamilton thought. "What hope do I have, God?"

The religious young man braced himself against the cold. It was nearing the end of February 1528. Hamilton glanced upward to see the top of St. Rule's tower being swallowed by the fog and freezing mist being whipped up off East Sands.

"Heretic! You deemed it acceptable for all to read the Word of God. You told others that prayers to the saints and the Blessed Virgin were wasted labor." Friar Campbell's voice began to rise. "You dismissed the worship of imagery, even the imagery of our holy saints! Heretic, I say!"

"I say no more than what Paul said," Hamilton said softly. "For there is one God, and one mediator also between God and men, and that is Christ Jesus."

The words of Scripture on the lips of the soft-spoken reformer enraged the panel of clerics. Hamilton had been preaching his reformist gospel to Scotland's flock for nearly a decade. When outraged Catholic officials had tried to silence him in the past, he had fled to Germany. But now he'd returned to stand in solidarity with those who believed as he did. Friar Campbell pounded the rail that surrounded Hamilton and his fellow reformers and shouted at the archbishop.

"My Lord, this man denies our holy institutions and the authority of the pope. I need accuse him no longer."

And indeed, he did not.

"We find that Patrick Hamilton has affirmed, published, and taught wicked heresies," the archbishop announced.

"Deliver him to the authorities for punishment and confiscate his possessions."

The tribunal rose and adjourned. Hamilton was led back to prison. From his cell, he watched as his inexperienced executioners hastily prepared a stake near the gate in front of St. Salvator's Chapel. The buildings of St. Andrews University loomed all around. All of them seemed to have been hewn from the same damp, ash-colored stone.

"I'll die tied to that cursed stake before another full day passes," Hamilton thought. He busied himself in prayer.

At noon the next day, the captain of the guard came for Hamilton. The prisoner strode stoically but with purpose to his own place of execution. He carried a copy of the New Testament. A few friends and supporters followed along.

When he got to the gate at St. Salvator's, Hamilton handed the Bible to one of his friends. He took off his hat and coat and gave them to another.

"These won't be of any good in the fire," Hamilton said.

Seeing the young man's defiance, the archbishop gave Hamilton one last chance to spare his life if he would take back what he had said during his brief trial.

He refused. "I will not deny my faith for awe of your fire," Hamilton said firmly. "Take me to the mercy of God."

A guard lashed Hamilton to the stake with an iron chain around his waist. The pile of wood and coals at his feet was sprinkled with gunpowder and set ablaze. The pile exploded briefly, scorching Hamilton's hand and cheek, then the fire went out. It was set again three times, but the fire would not catch.

"Have you really run out of dry wood and gunpowder?" wailed Hamilton, who was badly burned but far from fatally wounded. As his executioners searched for more fuel, Hamilton preached to the crowd gathered around him, urging them to repent.

At last, the guards managed to get the fire around Patrick Hamilton roaring. The chain that bound him turned red-hot and began to cut him in two. Death was near.

"Do you still hold to your word, heretic?" someone in the crowd shouted.

From within the swirling mass of flame and smoke, Hamilton raised three fingers on his badly charred hand, a sign of his faith in the holy trinity. "How long shall darkness overwhelm this realm?" the dying martyr shouted. "How long wilt thou suffer this tyranny of men?"

He kept his mangled hand raised until he was, mercifully, dead at last, one of dozens who would lose their lives in the cause of Reformation in the scenic seaside Scottish town of St. Andrews.

Like the deaths of many other warriors and martyrs, the sheer horror of Hamilton's execution made a lasting mark on St. Andrews, a place known far better today as the birthplace of golf than as the crucible for Protestant Christianity. Hamilton's spirit remains part of the lore in the town even five centuries after his death. Students and faculty at the University of St. Andrews continue to report strange crackling sounds and the persistent odor of burning flesh throughout the campus. Stones in the shape of Hamilton's initials, a "P" and "H," were laid into the spot where he was killed. It is well known among St. Andrews students that treading on the initials will result in a streak of bad luck.

Most striking, the image of Patrick Hamilton's face remains burned into the stone facade of the tower opposite where he was burned alive. Passers-by are warned not to look up at the jagged mask of horror, which appeared the day after his death. Even now, the charred face is visible in stark contrast to the massive expanse of smooth, gray rock.

Indeed Scotland is a study in such contrasts: of boulders and bogs; of sun-drenched meadows and fog-shrouded moors; of bloody battlefields and stellar golf courses. It is those golf courses that perhaps best define modern-day St. Andrews. In this place, known as the Home of Golf, lies the Old Course, the world's very first golf course, and by far the most famous. It is here in St. Andrews that the game established itself as a legitimate sport, where the first rules—most of which are still used today—were written, and where some of golf's first stars emerged.

It was also here that the Society of St. Andrews Golfers—later to become the Royal and Ancient Golf Club—was formed, the first governing body of golf. The Old Course has hosted the Open Championship more than any other venue.

Protestantism has its heroes and ghosts, and golf surely has its own. Their legends and their spirits intertwine like the ivy that covers St. Andrews's endless fieldstone walls. Old Tom Morris played St. Andrews's Old Course, tended to the links, and, in his shop adjacent to the 18th green, honed the craft of ball- and club-making. Willie Park excelled at St. Andrews, as did the second generation of greats, including their sons, Young Tom Morris and Willie Park Jr. Whenever any of these men took to the Old Course's first tee or walked off its 18th green, they could easily spot the Martyrs Memorial, a stone obelisk overlooking the sea that honors Patrick Hamilton and his fellow reformists.

And in the St. Andrews Cathedral graveyard, within sight of the spot where nearly five hundred years before,

Patrick Hamilton stood accused before the St. Andrews priory, there sits an oddly modern-looking tombstone. It sports the stone-carved image of a golfer in a sport coat and tam addressing his ball with a unique, open stance. The cathedral, once one of Europe's largest, has since been reduced to rubble by time, nature, and human conflict; it is the final resting place of Tommy Morris, the golf prodigy who also found both glory and tragedy at St. Andrews.

By the time Old Tom took the job as keeper of the green at the Old Course, his son Young Tom Morris, born in 1851, had already made a name for himself in the golf world by turning pro at the tender age of thirteen. In 1868, just after he turned seventeen, Tommy won his first Open Championship, a year after his father had won his last. Tommy won the next two as well and became the permanent keeper of the championship belt, a beautiful trophy made of red Moroccan leather with silver clasps. The tournament was not held in 1872 while the organizing committee figured out a way to thwart Tommy and find a new award for the winner. The decision was made to rotate the tournament over three courses, and from then on, the Claret Jug would be given to the winner, a tradition that lives on to this day.

In 1873 the Open was held again and Young Tom was the victor. He would never lift the trophy again.

In September 1875, Young and Old Tom Morris became embroiled in a high-stakes grudge match against brothers Willie and Mungo Park at the North Berwick course across the Firth of Forth from St. Andrews. The match pitted the two most dominant Scottish golfing families of the time against each other. Tensions ran high. Willie had won his fourth Open that year and Mungo had captured his first in 1874. The Parks began to attract a loud, unruly gallery of fans who weren't above kicking an opponent's ball back up the fairway or into a hazard.

Young Tom Morris knew he shouldn't have accepted the match. His wife, Margaret, was in her ninth month of a difficult pregnancy. But the look on his father's face when he begged his son to team up with him left Young Tom with little choice. He knew his father needed the 25 pounds wagered on the match to square the debt he owed the Parks from a loss earlier in the year. And the aging Morris needed a victory to silence a chorus of doubters who saw the Park family as the future of St. Andrews golf.

"What shall I do, Meg?" Young Tom had asked his wife.

She took his hand and placed it on her belly. "Go with your dad," she said, smiling. "Your work here is done."

And so he did. Father and son took the six-hour train and ferry ride around through Edinburgh and back east to North Berwick, a seaside town of one thousand people and a telegraph office. And now here he was, ready to play four nine-hole rounds at the North Berwick links course for the honor of his family.

Halfway through the match, the Morrises led by four holes. But when the third round began the next morning, their fortunes changed. Old Tom got wild with the driver and timid with the putter. His son, trying to make up for his father's missteps, began playing recklessly and the lead was whittled away. The growing gallery began to wave their fists and chant for the Park brothers.

In the final round, the pairs were neck and neck. The Parks went one up, then fell back to even. The tide seemed

to be turning in Old Tom's favor. Suddenly, while Young Tom
was busy playing out of a fairway bunker, Old Tom saw a
young man approaching from the adjacent fairway. At a full
run, the panicked messenger came up to Old Tom and delivered a dispatch from the local telegram office.

"Meg in labor," the telegram read. "Difficult birth. Come
home posthaste."

Old Tom stared at the note for several seconds. They
had a chance to go one up in the match with three to
play. If they left now, they would lose. And really, how
quickly could they get back to St. Andrews? The next train
to Edinburgh wasn't for several hours. The old man looked
up to see his son's shot land neatly on the green. As the
ball rolled to within four feet, he made a decision he would
regret the rest of his life. He folded the telegram and put
it in his pocket.

Old Tom and Tommy managed to rally on the second-
to-last hole and hung on to win the hotly contested match
by one stroke. As the gallery gave the winners a polite—if
slightly chilly—ovation, Old Tom pulled his son close.

"We've got to go now," he said. "Your wife is ill."

When one of the fans heard about Tommy's plight, he
volunteered his twenty-eight-foot ketch to sail the men
the thirty miles across the choppy Firth of Forth. The voy-
age took several hours, during which Old Tom drank porter
and engaged in nervous chatter with the crew while Tommy
paced the deck, fretting and staring out at the hills above
Fife.

At long last, the boat came alongside the stone pier at
St. Andrews. They were met by Tommy's younger brother,
Jimmy, who gave his father the awful news. It was up to Old
Tom to tell Young Tom.

"Tommy, it's over," the old man said. "Meg is dead. The baby is dead. I'm sorry."

Tommy was heartbroken, but the tragedy for the family was not over. Less than four months later, Old Tom found Tommy dead in his bed on Christmas morning at the age of twenty-four. It was often said that Tommy, torn by the loss of his beloved wife and unborn child, simply passed away because of the grief. However, his father disagreed.

"People say he died of a broken heart; but if that was true, I wouldn't be here either," the older man said.

Tommy was interred at the cathedral burial grounds in St. Andrews, and in 1878 a memorial was unveiled at his grave, including a life-size carving of Tommy. The inscription reads: "Deeply regretted by numerous friends and all golfers, he thrice in succession won the Championship belt and held it without envy, his many amiable qualities being no less acknowledged than his golfing achievements."

Just as many famous golfers lived, played, and passed away in and around the cradle of the game in St. Andrews, countless historic figures lived and died in pursuit of God and country here. Patrick Hamilton was far from the only religious figure martyred in St. Andrews during the reform, and his ghost is far from the only spirit haunting the ancient place. Hundreds of reformation martyrs were burned alive by the Catholic Church, their deaths forever marked in town, their ghosts still making their way down the cobbled streets.

The origin of St. Andrews itself is steeped in the macabre. Founded in the 1100s, the town is named for the patron saint of Scotland. St. Andrew, the brother of Simon Peter, was one of the original disciples of Jesus Christ and a successful evangelist in the early church. Andrew preached in Asia Minor and Macedonia, as well as southern Russia, where he was also the patron saint, winning over many converts before being martyred in Greece by a Roman governor who so feared Andrew that he crucified the apostle on a cross shaped like an X. The Scottish flag, a white X-shaped cross on light blue background—known as the Saltire, or St. Andrew's Cross—pays homage to St. Andrew's means of death. Andrew's bones were entombed in Greece for nearly three hundred years, until Constantine the Great moved them to Constantinople.

The connection to Scotland came when a Greek monk dreamed that he was to take St. Andrew's remains "to the ends of the earth." That monk, later known as Saint Rule, raided Andrew's tomb, taking a tooth, arm bone, kneecap, and fingers. For him the ends of the earth turned out to be the Scottish town of Kilrymont, where his boat wrecked upon the rocky coast. The remains were buried on a spot that became the site of the great cathedral in what is now the town of St. Andrews. Not surprisingly, the cathedral became a destination for pilgrims from all over the British Isles.

For centuries, the town was peaceful. It was, and is, a pleasant and welcoming place to visitors, with its many shops, pubs, and restaurants along the parallel Market, North, and South streets. St. Andrews Cathedral was built in 1160 over the remnants of a prior church. The grand cathedral was consecrated in 1318 by Bishop Wardlaw and King Robert the Bruce. Pope Benedict XIII officially recognized the place in 1413.

The University at St. Andrews, meanwhile, is the oldest college in Scotland and one of the finest institutions of higher learning in the British Isles. It counts many famous men and women among its graduates, including most recently Prince William, heir to the English throne.

As one would guess from its age and history, St. Andrews is the scene of many supernatural sightings. The ghosts include a friendly monk who helps visitors to the top of the treacherous stairs in St. Rule's tower, and the less amiable spirit of a friar who beckons tourists into the labyrinth of tunnels and stairways beneath the ruins of the church. All around the place, from the Castle Sands to the area around St. Rule's, visitors report feeling a strange presence and seeing the apparition of a murdered priest who continues to wander the property seeking peace.

As evidenced by Patrick Hamilton's brutal murder, for one bloody two-hundred-year period, St. Andrews was the epicenter of the English Reformation movement, which saw a large faction of disgruntled Catholics voicing displeasure over church politics and angrily breaking away from papal control. Part of a larger rebellion in the Church going on throughout Europe, the Reformation begat Protestant religion, but in that struggle the movement brought horror and death to the tiny Scottish village. The period is also at the heart of many of St. Andrews's supernatural tales.

The first victim of the Reformation in St. Andrews came in 1433, when Paul Craw, also known as Pavel Kravar, was burned at the stake for spreading the Bible translations of William Tyndale and John Wycliff, Englishmen considered heretics by the Roman Catholic Church for their revolutionary views. Legend has it that Craw was such an inspirational speaker that a brass ball was placed in his mouth by his executioners during the burning to prevent him from sermonizing to the witnesses who came to see his death.

A red stone cross is embedded on Market Street, marking the spot where Craw was killed.

George Wishart, a follower of Hamilton, was killed in December 1545. He was arrested by the Earl of Bothwell, acting on the orders of the infamously bloodthirsty Cardinal David Beaton. So fond of burning Protestants was Beaton that he would lean from the window of his quarters in St. Andrews Cathedral and applaud as his victims suffered and died. A quick trial ensued, and in March of the following year Wishart, too, was burned at the stake in St. Andrews. Before Wishart was murdered, he prophesized that the cardinal would come to an untimely end because of his actions.

The prediction came true two months later, when Beaton was slain in bed inside his castle by men avenging Wishart's brutal death. Legend has it that the cardinal was not immediately interred. "And so like a butcher he lived, and like a butcher he died, and lay seven months and more unburied, and at last like carrion was buried in a dunghill," reads one account of his end.

Not one to fade away quietly, the feisty Beaton haunts nearby Ethie Castle. His ghost is often seen in one narrow staircase that leads to a secret passage to his bedchamber. Visitors to Ethie Castle regularly hear footsteps and the scuffing noise of Beaton dragging his gouty leg around the haunted old place.

Henry Forrest became the next victim of the Reformation struggle in St. Andrews. He was jailed and charged with supporting Hamilton's views. During his incarceration, a friar was brought to his cell to hear his confession, during which Forrest reiterated his belief that Hamilton was a good man. The friar, who was loyal to the Catholic Church, used Forrest's words against him in court. Forrest was found "to be a heretic and to have an evil opinion of the faith; and therefore to be condemned and punished."

Two stories remain as to how Forrest died. One says that he was suffocated by his captors in his cell rather than burned at the stake, a move made so that his death would not incite repercussions from followers. The archbishop of St. Andrews had been advised by church leaders to stop the public killings, given that "the reek of Maister Patrik Hammyltoun has infected as many as it blew upon."

A more gruesome account, however, says Forrest was burned on the north side of the cathedral so the residents of Forfarshire could see the flames and take them as a warning against challenging the Catholic Church.

Walter Myln became the last martyr of the Scottish Reformation when he was burned at the stake in 1558 outside of Deans Court, which today houses research students at the university. In 1559, when the cathedral was sacked, wooden statues ripped from their places were burned at the site where Myln was executed. Myln, along with Wishart, Hamilton, and Craw, is among those honored on the Martyrs Memorial, visible from the Old Course.

Myln was not St. Andrews's last martyr, however. More than a century later, another prominent church leader was murdered. In 1679, Archbishop James Sharp was killed by covenanters near the present-day Magus Muir. His tomb is inside Holy Trinity Church on South Street. Sharp was aligned with the king of England and instrumental in establishing the Episcopal Church in Scotland. The covenanters continued to pursue the ideals of the Reformation of one hundred years earlier, forming the Presbyterian Church.

The covenanters who attacked Sharp were actually pursuing another victim but took advantage of the opportunity that Sharp presented, stabbing him to death while his horrified daughter looked on. Bishop John Paterson, notorious for inventing thumb screws for torturing those who backed the Reformation, preached at Sharp's funeral. Ever since, the ghost of Sharp and his noiseless carriage have been seen repeatedly at night making their way through St. Andrews.

Ghouls also lurk the main streets that run through the town from the cathedral to the Old Course and down to the sea. Several buildings in the town were used to dispose of plague victims in 1605. It's in and around those buildings that visitors and residents report seeing the ghost that has come to be known as the White Lady. Some claim she appears as a nun carrying a Bible. Others say she's more formally dressed in a flowing white dress and white gloves, perhaps the victim of a grave robber seeking vengeance. All agree she is wearing a veil and that she vanishes as quickly as she appears. The ghost is seen frequently in the evenings in October and November, wandering the grounds of the cathedral, or moving silently along St. Andrews's shoreline and around the fringes of the Old Course.

A legend has grown up around the veiled White Lady that claims she was a disfigured young woman who became a nun and kept her face covered out of shame. A glimpse of her hideous visage would drive the living insane, it is said.

The ghost of the White Lady would have been a familiar tale to Old Tom Morris, who, while he managed to keep his wits about him, was nonetheless visited by an inordinate number of personal tragedies. In addition to burying his famous son, Young Tom, this key player in the modern game of golf managed to outlive his four other children as well. The first passed away in 1850 at the age of four and the last in 1906.

Even his youngest son, John "Jack" Morris, who also earned his living in the game, could not escape the ill fate that seemed to haunt the famous family. Jack was up late one night in 1859 making golf balls at St. Andrews. He had taken up golf equipment manufacturing because a birth defect left him with legs too weak to play the game his father and brother excelled at. Despite his disability, however, he became known as an authority on the building, repair, and maintenance of all things golf. On this particular night, he appeared in perfect health when he told his family he was going to rest for the remainder of the evening. He was found a short time later in his bedchamber, dead from a sudden and quite massive heart attack.

Old Tom buried his youngest child. Some seventeen years later, his wife, Agnes, passed away as well.

In 1908, all alone at the age of eighty-nine, Old Tom succumbed to a fractured skull sustained when he mistook the cellar door for the lavatory door and fell down the stairs of the New Golf Club, located next to the 18th fairway of the Old Course in St. Andrews. He is buried next to Tommy in the St. Andrews Cathedral graveyard, two giants of the game resting eternally near the place where it all began.

Chapter 11

Ladies' Golf Club of Toronto: Where It's Always Ladies First

At the Ladies' Golf Club in Toronto, the men are welcome to play, but only during off-peak hours. And everyone has an equal chance of seeing the ghost that haunts the home of the club's famous founder. So haunted is the place that one member of the storied Gourlay golfing family has been hounded by ghouls since he worked at the course.

Ada MacKenzie ripped a perfect drive off the first tee, then strode with purpose down the fairway. She was officially in the hunt at the 1969 Ontario Senior Championship. From her athletic gait and trim figure it was impossible to tell she had just turned seventy-eight years old, by far the oldest competitor in the field.

"I started golfing when women were supposed to know more about a cookstove than a niblick," Ada joked with fans in her nasal, clipped delivery. She may have been a pioneer in her sport in her native Canada, but the Ontario Senior was just another day playing the game Ada MacKenzie loved.

Ada was born in Toronto on Halloween Day in 1891 to parents who were both affluent and passionate about golf. At twelve, she was sent off to Havergal College, a private girls' school that specialized in developing strong, empowered young women. She thrived in the school's challenging, competitive atmosphere, staying there until she was twenty. Ada developed incredible athletic prowess in sports ranging from basketball to tennis to ice hockey. But it was in golf that she found her real talent. After graduation she stayed on as an athletic instructor at Havergal, where she spent much of her free time fine-tuning her game.

By 1919 Ada was near the top of her form. That year she took the Duchess of Connaught Gold Cup and won the first of her five Canadian Women's Open Amateur championships. She came within two strokes of beating Glenna Collett in the U.S. Women's Open Amateur Championship in 1925. And in Canadian-only competition she was nearly unstoppable, finishing either first or second in the Canadian Ladies' Closed Championship every year from 1923 to 1933, the year she was named Canada's Female Athlete of the Year.

Even at the height of her career, Ada proved she was a well-rounded competitor. In 1926 she was named Canadian waltzing champion. She continued as a force in North American golf in the ensuing decades, posting victories in national tournaments in Canada throughout the 1940s and '50s. A savvy businesswoman who worked full time at a bank through most of her golf career, she also founded a women-only securities fund and designed a line of women's athletic clothing.

"Keeping active and busy has to be my key to success," Ada once told a reporter. "Some people have a tendency to over-indulge in sports. Not me. I treat athletics like recreation."

So full of energy was Ada that, as she took to the course on that sweltering late-summer day in 1969, few who knew her could have guessed that the Ontario Senior would be the last full round of golf in Ada's life. Two years later she was elected to the Canadian Golf Hall of Fame, and in 1973, at the age of eighty-one, Ada MacKenzie died peacefully one night not far from the golf club she founded in Toronto.

Her name remains alongside the greats in Canadian golf, but perhaps the most enduring legacy Ada created is the twenty-one-hole Ladies' Golf Club of Toronto on a stretch of old farmland in Thornhill, Ontario. In 1924, with $30,000 of her own money, financial backing from former Toronto Maple Leafs owner J. P. Bicknell, and a stellar layout by Canadian course designer Stanley Thompson, Ada founded a club that remains the only woman-owned golf club in North America. It is well known as a groundbreaking facility on the cause of women's golf.

It also seems like Ada got more than she bargained for when she purchased a house on the Thornhill property, a stately brick-faced home from which a previous tenant evidently never left. Almost since the place was founded, employees and guests—and perhaps even Ada herself— have seen visions of a ghostly old woman haunting various parts of the club. The legend maintains that the woman was the former owner of Ada's place. While it may be unnerving to some, it's also rather fitting that the chief specter at the Ladies' Golf Club, a place founded by a champion for female causes, would be a woman.

Such fair treatment for the fairer sex, however, was hardly on the mind of a former Ladies' Golf Club head professional. We'll call him Jasper. As he made his way into the clubhouse one evening, he came face to face with the ghost of the woman. It frightened him so badly that he went running full speed from the facility and was reluctant to ever go near the place again.

Even years later, Jasper had difficulty telling the story of the spirit that had frightened him so.

"I looked at his face and he was white," says David Gourlay Jr., who served as superintendent of the Ladies' Golf Club of Toronto in the mid-1980s. "It scared him to death. It was something he never wanted to see again.

"He hated going into that clubhouse," Gourlay adds.

Despite the dozens of stories like Jasper's from the myriad people who witnessed the ghostly old woman, Gourlay never did see her, but he also never doubted the truth of her existence. One of a long line of golf innovators, Gourlay knows firsthand the supernatural power that surrounds the game. For more than two centuries the name Gourlay has been well known throughout golf, both in North America and Great Britain. The family had their hands in every aspect of the game, from the making of golf balls to the care and maintenance of the links.

The Gourlays' connection to golf dates back to the 1790s, when Robert Gourlay and John Gunn advanced money to the town council of St. Andrews, Scotland, on the security of the links that is now known as the Old Course. Later Gourlay and Gunn exercised their right to sell the links, disposing of part of the land to Thomas Erskine. Then it was on to the making of golf balls, and by the mid-1800s, the Gourlay family was producing the highest quality and most costly feathery golf balls in Scotland, one of which is on display at the USGA Museum. A Dr. Graham, writing in 1848, even mentioned the Gourlay golf ball in a poem lamenting their cost and the fact they were not durable.

> Though golf be of our games most rare,
> Yet, truth to speak, the wear and tear

Of balls were felt to be severe
And source of great vexation.
When Gourlay's balls cost half-a-crown,
And Allan's not a farthing down,
The feck o's wad been harried soon,
In this era of taxation.

Then there was John Gourlay, who in the 1800s managed the Old Course at the Musselburgh Links in Scotland, where golf was played as early as the mid-1600s, and perhaps even earlier. Musselburgh was the birthplace of a number of famous inventions relating to golf, including the brass-soled club—or brassie—designed so golf balls could be played off a road that ran along the course. The 4.25-inch diameter hole was first adopted at Musselburgh as well.

Just about 150 years after their heyday as golf ball makers, a sect of the Gourlay clan made its way to Canada. David Gourlay emigrated from Scotland in 1948 and was a longtime superintendent on a number of Canadian courses. He also became a founding member of the Canadian Golf Course Superintendents Association. He passed on a love of the maintenance side of the game to his son, David Jr., who eventually found himself at Ada MacKenzie's beautiful, if slightly haunted, Toronto club.

Not long after a pale and shaken Jasper related his vision of the old woman's ghost, Gourlay moved on from the Ladies' Golf Club to nearby Eagle Creek Golf Club in Ontario to help complete that course's construction. During a span of about seven months, he lived in a house that was rented for him about a mile from the course. This, though, was not just another house—it was one with special traits and it started to display those talents shortly after Gourlay moved in.

"It was sort of backwards," says Gourlay, now chief operating officer at Colbert Hills Golf Club in Manhattan, Kansas, a course owned by Kansas State University, where his son Matt is the superintendent. "If I left the television on, when I came back, it would be off. If it was off when I left the room, I would come back in and it would be on. Same thing with the bathroom light."

At first Gourlay thought it might be a bad electrical system, but all of the wiring checked out OK. He resigned himself to living with a few switches that had minds of their own in an otherwise normal house. However, Gourlay could not have predicted, and was not prepared for, what came next.

One evening he invited Ken Skodacek and his wife over for a quiet evening of movie watching. Skodacek and former PGA Tour pro and television golf announcer Ken Venturi had designed the Eagle Creek course Gourlay was now growing in. Not long after the three sat down and flipped on the film, Gourlay heard music that seemed at first to be coming from outside.

No doubt a bunch of guys from his course construction crew had driven up, car stereo blasting, and were preparing to burst in looking to knock back a few beers or drag him out to a local watering hole. Gourlay panicked.

He bolted from his chair and rushed to the door to keep the hooligans from coming in. He knew that Skodacek and his wife were deeply religious people, not the type to entertain the idea of a night out with the boys.

But as he made his way through the kitchen, Gourlay realized the music wasn't coming from the street at all. It was coming from an adjacent bedroom. He stood transfixed, listening to the cacophony and watching as beams of light splayed from the gap between the door and the doorjamb of what should have been a dark room.

With his guests continuing to enjoy the movie and oblivious to the commotion, Gourlay turned the knob and walked into a scene he never could have imagined.

"All these toys were spinning in the room, lights going on all over the place, every toy was on. There was a fire truck on the table spinning," he says.

Gourlay claims there was no way anyone could have been playing a joke on him since the door was the only way into the room. There was a window—more like a piece of glass set into the wall—that looked out onto the yard, but it could not be opened. Plus, he adds, it was outside the realm of possibility that anyone could have snuck in.

"We were right in the next room," Gourlay maintains.

Not wanting to alert his guests, Gourlay handled the situation himself. "It kind of freaked me out. I turned off all the switches," having the most difficulty with the fire truck. "It was jammed on."

Gourlay returned to the living room and recounted the incident to the Skodaceks, who seemed unfazed by his account.

The next day Gourlay decided to revisit the room, which he believes was used as a children's bedroom by previous tenants who left behind the toys. He wasn't sure he had ever even set foot in the room before that night.

"This can't have happened," he thought.

He went back in and grabbed the toy fire truck first. The switch was jammed and he had a difficult time getting it to turn on. Once he did, Gourlay tried to get the truck to repeat its antics from the previous evening. "I put it on the table and it would spin and fall off, spin and fall off. The night before it spun like a top."

Gourlay is not the kind to be easily swayed by stories of ghostly old women, or by unexplained encounters with light switches and electric toys. While he may hail from Canada, Gourlay has a quality more akin to residents of Missouri.

"You've got to show me," he says with a grin.

And the spirits, on that night at least, had definitely shown him their presence. For those who think there might have been an outside influence of Gourlay's account of the evening's happenings, he dispels that idea.

"There was no drinking going on."

He also adds that the subject of that night's film had no role on his state of mind. "It was not a scary movie."

Gourlay may have been a bit freaked out, but he wasn't frightened enough by the experience to consider moving out of the house. He did, however, take a cue from numerous horror flicks, he says.

"I never looked in the mirror. If I was shaving in the morning, never. I told myself, 'Oh, God, don't look in the mirror,' and I never did."

The toys, for their part, remained silent and in darkness from then on, though the lights and television continued to turn on and off on their own. A few months later, Gourlay moved into a permanent residence, leaving the house behind but taking the memory of the bizarre encounter with him and keeping it to this day.

And back at the Ladies' Golf Club of Toronto, regulars and guests continue to witness the ghostly vision of the quiet old woman who haunts the late Ada MacKenzie's home course. Though Ada always wanted the place to be an attraction to new, inexperienced golfers, it seems that some of Thornhill's old-timers just can't bear to depart.

Chapter 12

Greg Norman: Golf's Most Famously Haunted Career

Golf is a cruel game. Just when you think you've come to embrace it, golf can break your heart like no lover ever could. In the annals of the sport, however, no one has ever had his hopes shattered as often and in such cruel ways as the dashing Aussie Greg Norman. It is not difficult to look back on his career and think that only a man eternally cursed by some dark entity could be forced to absorb so many soul-crushing defeats.

It can be said without a moment's hesitation that Greg Norman is one of the finest golfers ever to grace the world's fairways.

In the age of persimmon woods and balata golf balls, he was known to be one of the longest and straightest hitters. He combined that with a steely resolve that resulted in sixty-seven tournament victories around the world—including twenty on the PGA Tour—and two major titles. Seven times between 1986 and 1997 he finished the year ranked number one in the world, and three times over that same span he was ranked second. He is the only player ever to have held top ranking in both the PGA Tour and the European PGA Tour.

Norman was born on February 10, 1955, in Mount Isa, a mining town in the interior of the Australian state of Queensland. Like many kids his age in the area, he initially took to rugby and cricket. He started playing golf when he turned sixteen, becoming a scratch player within a year. He became a pro under the tutelage of Charlie Earp at the Royal Queensland Golf Club pro shop, making about $30 a week as he learned his way around the game that would become his livelihood. At age twenty-one he won the 1976 West Lakes Classic at The Grange in Adelaide, South Australia, to capture his first pro title.

Norman didn't just have the game; he had the looks as well. Tall and lean, with a head of flowing white hair usually topped with his trademark wide-brimmed straw hat, he struck an imposing figure striding down the fairways stalking another victory, all the while oozing confidence seasoned with just the right hint of arrogance. His smile could illuminate a small city, and all of this was before he uttered a sound. When Norman did speak, his words were bathed in that Australian accent that sealed his status as a near mythic figure: Women melted and men were envious.

Yet despite the success he found on the golf course, despite the millions of dollars earned, the legion of loyal fans, the iconic stature he achieved in a game full of extra-large personalities, it could be easily argued that Norman was cursed. And not simply because he lost a few high-profile tournaments.

Almost any person who has taken up a golf club—from the weekend hacker to the most successful pro—can point to games or tournaments where victory was easily within his grasp but in the end proved elusive. The defeats, more often than not, were the result of something the golfer did—a slice off the fairway, an approach shot knocked down by a low-hanging branch, a hiccup on a putting stroke that left the ball two inches short of the hole.

However, with Norman, it is not difficult to look back at his career and think some sinister, external force was working against him, keeping him from sitting in the pantheon of golfing greats alongside Ben Hogan, Sam Sneed, and Arnold Palmer.

Known as the Great White Shark in a nod to his Australian heritage as well as his tenacity on the course, Norman finished second eight times in the four majors—Masters, U.S. Open, the Open Championship (referred to as the British Open in the United States), and the PGA Championship—the only man to hold that distinction. But it was more than just numbers. It was the cruel and painful way that fate played with Norman. Twice he was defeated when unheralded foes holed miraculous shots to grab the only major victories of their careers. Other times his downfall was an excruciatingly long self-inflicted implosion. His final-round performances on occasion were dismal, many times the result of unsteady putting.

Of the eight occasions he finished second in golf's most important tournaments, five were at the hands of players for whom it would be their first and only major. On the other three occasions, the losses came to players for whom the title would be their last major. In one of those, the 1986 Masters, at the age of forty-six Jack Nicklaus became the oldest player to capture that particular event, a mark that still stands. That year Norman had led all four majors going into Sunday's round—an accomplishment known derisively as the "Norman Slam." He managed to win only the Open Championship that season.

Watching the variety of ways that Norman stumbled, fell, or was vanquished would knot the stomach of even the most seasoned golf fan. Golfers fail all the time. Every weekend during golf season, the television shows us the one and only player who had what it took to win—and the dozens who came up short. Norman's fate, however, frequently seemed to be dictated by an outside hand. He was like a marionette controlled by a puppeteer with a cruel streak and a dark heart.

The worst and most excruciating was his last grasp at a major. The golfing world watched as he impaled himself in the 1996 Masters, denying himself one last time the green jacket he so coveted. Norman began that tournament with a clarion call to the rest of the field in what the *New York Times* said was "a flawless 63" in the first round. There were other scores in the 60s that day, but not one of the other golfers played as well as Norman, who became the first player to have two 63s in majors. His first came during the second round of the 1986 Open Championship at Turnberry, which he won.

In Augusta in 1996, Norman followed his stellar opening with a round of 69 on Friday and a 71 in tough conditions on a Saturday that saw Nick Faldo shoot 73 and eventual third-place finisher Phil Mickelson notch a 72. Norman's lead was six shots heading into Sunday.

Mickelson was asked that Saturday if Norman could be caught. "I don't know, what do you think?" he answered, then unknowingly foreshadowed the conclusion. "Anything's possible, so I don't want to rule out the improbable."

Masters Sunday in 1996 was a beautiful day—the sun shone and the wind was all but still, a perfect day for scoring. No one could have foreseen that such an idyllic moment in time would long be remembered for tragedy rather than triumph.

The tide turned for Norman on the first shot of the first hole when he pulled his golf ball into the trees and made a bogey. By the time he was done with the front nine, the lead was down to two shots as playing companion Faldo, already the winner of two Masters and two Open Championships, forged a solid round.

Once Norman made the turn, he continued his erratic play on the back nine, recording bogies at 10 and 11 and allowing Faldo to move into a tie for the lead.

Then came the dreaded 155-yard 12th hole, called Golden Bell, with its shallow green guarded by a stream in front and a nasty bunker and azalea-covered bank behind. What makes the hole most treacherous are the swirling winds in the part of the Augusta National Golf Club known as Amen Corner. They seem to defy prediction or logic. Perhaps those winds are manipulated by the ghost of the legendary Bobby Jones, founder of Augusta, or of Clifford Robinson, the man who guided Jones's dream from 1934 to 1976, until finally, in failing health, he committed suicide on his beloved course.

Whatever the cause, the wind played a role and Norman's tee shot landed on the banking in front of the narrow green, trickling slowly and painfully back into Rae's Creek. A gasp was heard across the course and in the millions of homes where the television was tuned to the drama. During Friday's round, when the gods were with him, Norman's tee shot landed and stayed on the same bank and he made par; Sunday it was a double bogey. Faldo made 3, taking a lead he would never relinquish.

The two matched each other over the next three holes, with both scoring two birdies each, but any hope of a Norman resurrection vanished at the final par-3 as he hooked his tee shot into the water on the 16th while Faldo made another par.

Following the round, perhaps jaded so much by his other near misses, it was as if Norman was immune to the stunning collapse, saying he was not particularly injured by the loss.

"I have a strong belief that something good is going to happen to me before my career is over."

His belief may have been strong, but his prediction was incorrect. His spell had been broken. He would win two more times on the PGA Tour and come near the top at one more Masters and two Open Championships, but the ultimate glory of taking home a major would never happen again. Perhaps Norman should have known better. The 1996 Masters defeat wasn't the beginning of his bad luck, it was just the latest in a long streak of misery. Norman's tragic history really began to unfold twelve years earlier in Mamaroneck, New York, at the legendary Winged Foot Country Club.

In 1984 Norman was making a name for himself in the United States, having captured his first PGA Tour title after years of racking up a number of victories on the European and Australian tours. So it was not a complete shock when Norman was paired against Fuzzy Zoeller in an eighteen-hole playoff for the U.S. Open title. Norman must have felt the golfing gods had smiled on him when, on the 72nd hole the previous day, he sank a forty-foot par putt to thrust himself into the playoff. The luck that was with him on Sunday did not carry over to Monday, however, and the curse, unbeknownst to anyone including Norman himself, had begun.

The playoff was over early as fate looked kindly on Zoeller. Fuzzy canned a sixty-eight-foot putt on the second hole for birdie while Norman three-putted for a double bogey. Norman repeated the dismal effort on the greens at the 3rd and 5th holes with two more three-putts; from there the outcome was academic. The loss marked Norman's first in a string of dubious records that would haunt him throughout his career. Zoeller set the eighteen-hole playoff margin of victory at eight, carding a 67 while Norman staggered home with a 75.

That was Norman's first real shot at a major, and his Monday performance on one of golf's biggest stages was attributed to his inexperience. Surely, everyone thought, he would have his share of major trophies when all was said and done.

Two years later Norman created the infamous "Norman Slam" by blowing a third-round lead in three of four majors. Still, he won the fourth, the 1986 Open Championship at Turnberry, in convincing style, besting the field by five shots. He had his first major under his belt. The three defeats, though, grabbed their share of attention. Norman lost the Masters to Jack Nicklaus by one stroke, needing only a par on the 18th to force extra holes. Instead, he hit his approach shot from the middle of the fairway into the gallery right of the green on the way to a bogey after a stunning Nicklaus-like charge, in which he made birdies on holes 14, 15, and 16.

The tragic spiral continued for Norman in the U.S. Open thanks to another collapse in the final round. He shot 75 and dropped from first to twelfth, as Raymond Floyd, forty-three, became the oldest winner of that event, a record later surpassed by Hal Irwin. But it was at the PGA Championship a few weeks later in Toledo, Ohio, that Norman might have felt for the first time there was a force from deep within the universe working against him. Norman dominated play at the Inverness Club, leading the field all three days. He had a four-shot advantage over Bob Tway with eight holes to go. Tway was in just his second year on the PGA Tour and had already garnered three titles earlier that year. Despite his success, there were few who thought the young Tway could stand up to the world's top-ranked golfer.

Tway and Norman were in the final group, and the first sign for Norman that something was amiss came on the 11th hole, when he piped a drive down the middle of the fairway that somehow came to rest in one of the few—possibly only—unrepaired divot holes. His approach from the poor lie plugged in a bunker and he made a double-bogey 6.

Tway kept chipping away at Norman, and when they walked onto the 18th tee, they were tied. The advantage immediately shifted to Norman, who found the center of the fairway off the tee while Tway knocked his first shot into the gnarly, penalizing rough—advantage Norman. When Tway's approach from the thick grass plopped into a green-side bunker, Norman seemingly had the tournament in his grasp, but his approach wedge, which initially found the putting surface, spun back off the green into thick rough. It was difficult to imagine that the advantage did not still belong to the best player in the world, but that was shattered when Tway drove a dagger through Norman's heart by holing his bunker shot from twenty-five feet for a birdie. Norman needed a chip-in to tie, but that went well past the hole and he missed the comeback putt for good measure. finishing with a miserable 76.

Norman was now part of another forgettable record as Tway became the first man to win the PGA Championship with a birdie on the final hole since the format changed to medal play in 1958; prior to that it had been match play.

The hand that denied Norman that last major of the 1986 season did the same in the first of the 1987 campaign when Augusta native Larry Mize holed a 140-foot pitch shot on the second playoff hole of the Masters to stun Norman once again and cement the view that a dark cloud followed him in the four most important tournaments of the year.

Mize and Seve Ballesteros shot 71s on the final day of the Masters and Norman a 72 to qualify for the playoff. On the first extra hole, Ballesteros was eliminated, sending Mize and Norman to the difficult par-4 11th, where the green is guarded on the left by water. Mize approached first and his uninspired effort left him ninety feet short of the putting surface. Norman knocked his shot to fifty feet from the pin, a safe play, and surely he must have thought that soon he would be inside Butler Cabin slipping on the green jacket. Standing at his ball Norman could only watch in stunned silence as Mize's pitch shot found the bottom of the cup, sending him into a leap-filled frenzy. When order was restored, Norman's bid to tie the hole slid past the cup.

"I'm more disappointed now than any tournament I've lost," he said shortly afterward.

After a calm 1988, where he at least did not make news for how he lost, Norman would find a new way in 1989 to finish second in a major. The Open Championship was at Royal Troon that year, and on Sunday Norman produced a round for the ages. Starting the day six shots off Wayne Grady's lead, he birdied the first six holes on the way to a course record 64 and a four-day total of 275, a number equaled by fellow Australian Grady and American Mark Calcavecchia. The three then teed it up for the first four-hole playoff in Open history. Coming to the 18th hole, Calcavecchia and Norman were tied for the lead, two shots ahead of Grady.

Then, incredibly, Norman disintegrated, but seemingly not by his own device.

Norman had oftentimes been criticized for being too brash and daring on the course when a conservative approach was best, but the charge could not be leveled against him that day. Looking to play it safe on his tee shot, Norman elected to go with a three-wood rather than a driver in order to come up short of a nasty fairway bunker. His crushed tee shot went farther than anyone could imagine and he watched helplessly as the white sphere bounded along the rock-hard links turf, traveling yards beyond what he'd intended, not stopping until it came to rest in the exact sandy quagmire he was looking to avoid. Not only did the ball find sand, but it also came to rest so close to the front face that Norman was prevented from going for the green. His recovery effort from the difficult lie found another bunker closer to the green; the next shot was disastrous.

Calcavecchia was already on the putting surface in two, and Norman knew he had to get there as well with his next shot if he was to have any chance of prolonging the playoff. Norman misfired so badly that the ball ended up out of bounds on the clubhouse grounds, up against the leg of the caddymaster. His humiliating conclusion to the collapse came when he picked up his golf ball and did not finish out, recording no score for the playoff. Calcavecchia birdied 18 for his first and only major.

In 1990 there were no major losses, but Norman was felled in regular PGA Tournaments by two of the best-remembered shots of the decade. First, Robert Gamez holed a seven-iron from the middle of the fairway to win at Bay Hill with host Arnold Palmer looking on. The spot from which the shot was taken is commemorated with a plaque. A few weeks later at

New Orleans, David Frost jarred a fifty-foot bunker shot on the final hole of the tournament to beat Norman by one. What was even more heartbreaking about that defeat was that moments before, Norman had stood up to the pressure, firing a sensational two-iron to within two feet of the hole, guaranteeing a birdie. However, after Frost's shot, the heroic effort was for naught. Even when Norman did everything right, things went wrong.

For the next few years Norman dominated golf but did not contend in a major championship. Then in 1993, after dismal performances in the first two majors of the year, Norman seemed to rid himself of his demons, capturing the Open Championship at Royal St. George's by two shots over Nick Faldo.

So when the Tour returned to Inverness—the sight of his stunning 1986 loss to Tway—for the PGA Championship a few weeks later, Norman was the favorite. Many thought this would be an opportunity to exorcise a horrible memory. This time Norman's game held up through seventy-two holes, finishing tied for the lead with Paul Azinger. Norman's four rounds in the 60s, coupled with his four rounds in the 60s at Royal St. George's, made him the first player to accomplish the remarkable feat. He had entered the final round with a lead of one and shot 69, but Azinger turned in a stellar round of 68 to force the playoff.

This heartbreak added a different confidence-shaking twist. On the first playoff hole, Norman's birdie putt for the win appeared to be in the cup, then inexplicably spun out as if nudged by an unseen hand of doom. On the second play-off hole, Norman needed a five-footer for par to tie Azinger, who was already in, but his effort was a repeat of the previous hole. The ball appeared to fall but then somehow worked its way out. Azinger took home the title, the only major of his career, and another chapter was written into Norman's book of horrors that had yet to be completed.

Two years later at the U.S. Open, as Sunday dawned over the Shinnecock Hills Golf Club, the scenario was one that had been repeated so many times: Greg Norman was leading a major. The logical question that followed was: What cruel blow would fate deal him this time?

The answer came in the form of a balky putter. He made one birdie on Sunday, his only one of the weekend, and watched as diminutive Corey Pavin lifted the trophy, for the only major of his career.

"It never haunts me," he said of the loss. Few, if any, fans, journalists, or players believed him. How could he not be affected by so many close calls, so many crushing, seemingly inexplicable losses?

As Norman aged and became less competitive on the PGA Tour, he entered fewer and fewer tournaments, preferring to concentrate on his highly successful wine and course-design businesses, which appear to be immune from his bad luck. However, in 2008, at the age of fifty-three, the Shark found himself with a renewed interest in competitive golf, in part because he was now eligible for the PGA Champions Tour and his new wife, tennis great Chris Evert, encouraged him to play more tournaments. In May of that year, he entered the PGA Senior Championship, a major, and played three solid but not spectacular rounds. Entering Sunday, he was five shots off the lead and gave himself virtually no chance to win. After a consistent eleven holes at the extremely difficult Oak Hill Country Club, Norman ignited the crowd, playing the next five holes in 4 under par, thrusting himself into contention. Stepping onto the tee of the par-4 17th,

Norman remarkably was just one shot from the top. Two pars on the way in would make a formidable statement, forcing those on the course to play nearly flawless golf the rest of the way.

Then, as it had so many times before, Norman's world crashed and burned, another stroll down his memory lane of horrors.

First he hit a poor drive into the right rough and an even worse second shot into the left rough, all on his way to a double bogey. He followed that up with a bogey on the 18th. Had he merely parred the final two holes, Norman would have found himself in a playoff with eventual champion Jay Haas.

The tone Norman exhibited after the round was one of a man whose desire for victory was sapped, all those defeats perhaps having finally taken their toll.

"I always thought I was too far behind the leaders and it didn't make any difference," he said of his poor finish, a remarkably offhand comment from a man who had made his share of Sunday charges.

Then in July 2008, Norman entered the Open Championship at Royal Birkdale, on the windswept coast of northwest England. Nobody gave the two-time winner of the event any hope of taking home the Claret Jug, least of all Norman. So when he finished the first round with a 70, one shot behind the leaders, there was little cause to think him a serious contender, even when he backed it up with another 70 on Friday to stay firmly in the hunt, just one shot behind the triumvirate of leaders. Then on Saturday, with winds gusting to over 40 mph—conditions better suited to younger, hardier men than Norman—he carded a remarkable 2-over-par 72 and moved into first place, two shots ahead of defending champion Irishman Padraig Harrington and the Korean K. J. Choi.

Sunday predictions called for a drop in winds but the weather prognosticators were wrong, and again the winds whipped off the North Atlantic, dropping temperatures and raising the level of difficulty. So brutal were conditions that many surmised the course was playing, even for these seasoned professionals, some five shots over par. Surely this would not be Greg Norman's day, and when he struggled early on, bogeying the first three holes, then the sixth, to drop out of the lead, it looked as if he would once again be brushed aside by the golf gods. Then, what no one could have predicted knowing Norman's past happened: The ghosts of golf smiled on him. Tournament leader Harrington bogied the 7th through 9th holes while Norman made three pars. The result: He was back on top by a shot and merely nine holes away from the most improbable major tournament victory ever.

Alas, the fairytale was over a short time later. The horror tale that has been so often repeated was again the story for Norman. He reeled off bogies on the back nine, not unexpectedly. But while that was happening, his playing partner, Harrington, was turning in one of the most remarkable closing runs in major tournament history, playing as if the wind was not a factor. He carded a 32 on the back to win by two shots over Ian Poulter and four over Norman, who finished in a tie for third.

A week later and a little to the north, Norman made a run at the Senior Open Championship at Troon Golf Club in Scotland, but he faltered late and was never a real threat on Sunday. Following his round he acknowledged that what had happened over the past two weeks might have been out of his control. Maybe, just maybe, this was his acknowledging that much of his past had been decided by an unseen and, perhaps, sinister force.

"The golfing gods were just not on my side over the past couple of weeks," he said, articulating what many golf observers had thought for years.

It is not difficult to look back and not think that somewhere, for some unknown reason, one of the finest players of all time had a black mark next to his name and, cursed or not, the fate of Greg Norman, on so many occasions, was decided for him.

Chapter 13

Hilton Head: Ghost of the Blue Lady

For golfers, Hilton Head, South Carolina, is a little slice of low-country heaven. There might be only twenty courses on the island but they are some of the country's finest. Mix in the unique cuisine and the hospitality of its inhabitants, and it's easy to see why the island is such a popular destination. But like any place with a rich history, Hilton Head harbors its share of dark tales and mystery.

Adam Fripp could tell the weather was about to sour. From the looks of the southern sky, they had maybe a day to prepare for the coming gale.

A storm had formed west of Jacksonville, Florida, and was gathering strength for its short, destructive journey. It was first declared a tropical storm in the early hours of August 30, 1898. Within just six hours, it was a full-fledged hurricane bearing down on the wind- and sea-swept low country of Hilton Head, South Carolina.

Adam had been the keeper of the lighthouse at Hilton Head for three years. The widower had stocked up on oil to keep the lamp burning as a warning to ships, and he'd squirreled away the necessary provisions to sustain himself and his twenty-year-old daughter, Caroline, through the storm season. The old man busied himself one more time, checking every window and door in the 136-foot structure. A day later the hurricane slammed into Hilton Head packing 100-mph winds. It made nary a scratch in the old lighthouse.

Adam Fripp and his daughter had made it through another storm.

Adam relaxed a little, though he knew full well the storm season was just gearing up. He had to stay on guard. His vigilance paid off as two more hurricanes skirted the coast and two more tropical storms soaked Hilton Head to its core. The light shone bright and Adam and Caroline remained safe in the lighthouse-keeper's home, despite the foul weather.

By September 25, 1898, the peak of the busy storm season had passed, but Adam still cast a wary eye toward the ocean as reports came in of a tropical storm forming near the West Indies. The gale tracked slowly, methodically northwest, churning the seas and becoming a hurricane as it hit Cuba, Puerto Rico, and Haiti. By 6 p.m. on October 1, the massive storm, with winds approaching 150 mph, was heading straight for Hilton Head. Adam had never seen a storm of this magnitude and was frightened not just for his daughter and for himself, but also for the ships he knew would be caught in the swirling hell. Days before the storm arrived, it was already bringing rain like he had never seen, pelting the lighthouse windows like a barrage of so many small stones. The barometer dropped precipitously. He and Caroline braced themselves for the most frightening experience of their lives.

The beast of a storm made landfall on October 2 near Brunswick, Georgia, with Hilton Head north of the eye, caught in the ripping, counterclockwise winds being fed by the warm water of the Gulf Stream.

The windows in the lighthouse blew out and the light turned to dark. Adam's first thought was to get the fire going again. He was racing to the light in the howling wind and driving rain blowing in through the spoiled windows when a fierce pain gripped him. Just feet from the stairs leading up to the light, he clutched at his heart and fell to the soaked floor.

"Keep the lamp lit," he told Caroline before his heart gave out and he was dead.

Granting him his final wish, she left her father there on the floor and climbed the rain-slick stairs in the driving gale. Fighting her way to the top, she managed to reignite the flame, which stayed lit for the remainder of the deadly hurricane. The exhaustion and grief took their toll on poor Caroline, however. A few weeks later, she fell ill and died. The father and daughter who had battled so bravely to keep ships safe off Hilton Head were buried together nearby. Their graves are a constant reminder of the darker side of this scenic paradise. Caroline was buried in her favorite blue cotton dress. Few who knew her in life would have guessed that in death she was destined to become one of Hilton Head's most famous residents.

Today Hilton Head Island is better known as a golf resort and beachfront getaway than as a hazard to navigation that requires protection in foul weather. Golf came to Hilton Head Island in the late 1950s, kicking off a trend that continues to this day. Sea Pines opened in 1961, but it was the Harbour Town Golf Links, with its distinctive red-and-white striped lighthouse that is the area's most celebrated layout. It was here that architect Pete Dye changed the golf world in 1969. For at least twenty years before Dye's stunning work, golf design was dominated by Robert Trent Jones, whose repetitive style stuck strictly to the penal school of architecture;

shots hit off line are the only ones penalized. Jones put a premium on long and straight. Dye's work, meanwhile, hearkened back to the roots of thoughtful architecture. His layouts conjure images of the 1920s and 1930s when his predecessors—Charles Blair Macdonald, Donald Ross, A. W. Tillinghast, and others—rewarded golfers for the strategic play and accurate shot-making.

The lengthy roster of course creators around Hilton Head reads as an impressive who's who in the golfing industry. It includes Dye, Jack Nicklaus, Arthur Hills, Arnold Palmer, Tom Fazio, Rees Jones, Gary Player, and of course, Trent Jones himself. Along with their talent for design, the architects were all fortunate enough to be able to work with a malleable canvas of windswept, low-country landscape on which to create their visions.

But as the tale of Caroline and Adam Fripp reminds us, all is not always bright and sunny on Hilton Head. Stories abound that reveal the island's dark side. In recent decades, Caroline's ghost has been seen wandering the area. Especially during hurricane season, her spirit can be seen wandering near the lighthouse or around the old keeper's home, still wearing the blue dress she was buried in. In part because of her dress, and in part because of her great sadness, she has come to be known on Hilton Head as the Blue Lady. Her ghostly presence serves to remind islanders of the power of the wind and the sea.

Among the first to witness the spirit were a young couple, both seniors at Hilton Head Preparatory School, who wandered hand-in-hand down a local lovers' lane in Harbour Town. The students had no idea the old building at the end of the road was the lighthouse-keeper's house where Caroline had died. The building had been moved from Leamington to the Sea Pines area in 1967. They may have been looking for romance, but what they found instead was the Blue Lady. Caroline's ghost appeared before them dressed in sheer blue and bathed in an eerie glow.

The teens ran home, where the boy told his parents about the face-to-face encounter with the ghost. Four adults drove back to the site looking to prove that there was nothing supernatural going on. As they inspected the area around the house, one of the men screamed. There in an upstairs window of the old place was Caroline in all her blue, shimmering glory.

Right before their eyes, she floated over to the door and onto the front porch.

"A Blue Lady," one of them whispered to the other. The name stuck.

For many years local residents kept the story of the Blue Lady to themselves, though they swore she was real. The boy who had at first been so frightened by Caroline's ghost struck up a sort of odd friendship with the specter. He frequently visited the home and she never failed to appear, he claims.

Finally, construction in the area resulted in several buildings, including the old lighthouse-keeper's home, being significantly altered. Since then she has never again appeared to her young male student admirer.

In addition to those who have seen the Blue Lady drifting along the shoreline, many others have heard her sobbing late into dark nights in early fall. Perhaps she still grieves the passing of her beloved father, or perhaps the Blue Lady sheds tears for all those sailors who lost to the hurricanes of the Atlantic.

But not all of Hilton Head's supernatural activity can be attributed to the Blue Lady. At the Harbour Town Lighthouse there have been a number of reports of a cold chill that envelops tourists who have visited the landmark since it opened in 1970. Many believe the ghost is that of a Yemassee Indian who died in a battle just as Europeans began arriving en masse on the Carolina shores.

A tipping point for the survival of the people colonizing the area occurred in 1715. Years earlier the Yemassee had clashed with the Spanish governor in what is now Georgia and relocated near the mouth of the Savannah River. Angered by British practices such as slavery, the whipping of Indians, and the theft of their land, the Yemassee launched a small war on the colonists in 1712 and then a full-scale uprising in 1715.

Tribes united to battle the English, inflicting heavy losses and causing many of the settlers in the territory to abandon their homes and retreat to Charlestown, where starvation soon became a problem as supplies ran low. The tide of the conflict turned, though, in 1716 when the Cherokee sided with the colonists and began to attack the powerful Creek Indians. The last battles were fought in 1717 before a fragile peace was restored. Perhaps it was then that the ghost of the Yemassee warrior began his eternal journey.

Another spirit making its home in the Hilton Head area is that of William Baynard, who is said to haunt the family mausoleum in the Zion Cemetery, which sits between the Port Royal Golf Resort and the Palmetto Hall Golf Club.

William Baynard was a character. The son of William Thomas Baynard, he inherited the adjoining Spanish Wells Plantation and Muddy Creek Plantation. William married Catherine Adelaide Scott in 1829 and the couple had four children. Legend has it that William's facility for poker led to him winning the deed to the one-housand-acre Braddock's Point Plantation in 1840.

Later he would buy the Davenport House in Savannah that was later turned into a museum. It was William who also commissioned the building of the grand Baynard Mausoleum, and it is said that it is his funeral procession that can be seen on the darkest of nights passing the ruins of his plantation on Braddock's Point or the mausoleum that bears his family's name.

While there may be plenty of surf, sun, and world-class golf to be had on Hilton Head, there's also an impressive collection of spirits haunting the place for reasons known only to them. And on a stormy, low-country fall night, it's easy to imagine that all of the ghosts of Hilton Head are flying and howling on the ocean breeze.

Chapter 14

Death Messages: Golf Course Encounters from Beyond the Grave

Many fantastic and unexplainable occurrences have happened on golf courses. The most strange, perhaps, occur when the dead decide it is there that they'll reach back into the mortal world. Here are three such stories.

For more than forty years, Michael Blair and Dai Davies were friends, drawn together by their love of rugby, golf, and one country in particular.

"I'm a Welshman, born and bred. I'm a proper Welshman and I live in England. Dai is a Welshman by preference, born in England of English parents," Michael says. In fact, in his zeal to become an honorary Welshman, Davies changed his first name in the 1970s from David to Dai, the Welsh version of the moniker.

The two met at the Sutton Colfield Rugby Club in 1964. Dai was still playing the game, while Michael had hung up his cleats. Later the two would be united on the sports staff of the *Birmingham Post*, Dai arriving a few years after Michael. Eventually Dai became the golf correspondent with Michael, the editor of the sports section and Dai's boss. That did not stand in the way of a deep and long-lasting bond.

"We drank together. We laughed together and we shared a love of golf," Michael says. "It was natural that we played a lot of golf together," something they did even after Dai left the *Post* in 1982 to become the golf correspondent for the *Guardian* newspaper.

Dai's father was also a journalist and a golfer.

"He gave him a love and respect for the game," says Michael.

Dai and Michael played all over the British Isles as well as in the United States, where they took their game to the courses of Pinehurst, throughout South Carolina and into Florida.

In 1997 the aging Dai was made to retire from his full-time position, a year later than was normally mandated. The paper kept him on so he could anchor the coverage of the Ryder Cup. Even when he did finally hang it up, Dai kept working for the *Guardian* as a contract writer.

Though Michael and Dai had many shared likes and passions, one of their more bitter disagreements was over their respective home courses. Michael, a low single-digit handicap in his prime, played his golf out of Moor Hall Golf Club in Warwickshire, while Dai, who played in the low double digits, teed up at Whittington Heath Golf Club in Lichfield; a drive of about twenty minutes separates the two.

"Moor Hall is a much more attractive golf course, but substantially easier," Michael contends. "And he never let me forget that."

Whittington was also the scene of one of their more memorable disagreements. "He once grossly offended me," Michael adds with a chuckle. The insult came as a result of a shot he played that Dai was sure would find one of Whittington's bunkers. Much to Dai's dismay, however, the ball skirted past that hazard unscathed, raising his ire.

"He called me a jammy Welsh bugger," Michael says with feigned incredulity. "I held it against him for the rest of his days."

Even though he was the better golfer, Michael always had a difficult time playing Whittington Heath. That is, he did, until a round in May 2008 that he will never forget.

Michael was part of the Moor Hall senior team that was up against Whttington. Dai, who had been sick for some time, was not participating, but on the first tee his name came up.

"I happened to ask the opposition if they knew Dai, and they said they did," Michael remembers. "I asked if they knew he was ill and they did not."

Michael told the group that Dai was in a local hospice and asked if it was far from the course—he was planning on stopping in to see his friend after the round—to which came the reply, "wait until we get to the second tee."

A few minutes later they arrived at the spot and the hospice was easily visible from there. "Across a field to the left of the village church," Michael recalls. "That's where the old boy was laying."

It was then that Michael began a remarkable streak. First, he birdied the par-4 2nd hole, followed with pars on the par-4 3rd and par-3 4th, and dropped a forty-footer for a birdie on the difficult par-4 5th. He looked forward with glee to recounting his accomplishments to his old friend and showing him the scorecard that read, in part, 3-4-3-3.

With his round over, Michael and his opponents were in the clubhouse sitting down to lunch when they received news on Dai.

"He's gone," were the words Michael and the others heard. It was then that he realized with amazement that when his longtime friend had passed away, "I could have well been on the course."

It is not hard to imagine that somehow Dai had a hand in the day's events and, if nothing else, at least witnessed them. Michael never had a chance to brag in person to Dai about his remarkable run of holes, but to this day maintains that "Spiritually, I did."

It is an indelible image cast into the memory of any golf fan who has ever seen it. The legendary Ben Crenshaw bent over at the waist, his head in hands, engulfed in tears as caddy Carl Jackson reaches to embrace him seconds after Crenshaw's putt dropped to give him the 1995 Masters title. The entire world watched this release of emotion for Crenshaw, who the Sunday of Masters week had found out that his teacher and mentor, Harvey Penick, had died after a long illness. That Wednesday Crenshaw and fellow PGA Tour great Tom Kite flew to Austin, Texas, to act as pallbearers for the Penick funeral, then flew back for the next day's first round.

The week before the tournament, Crenshaw had visited Penick in the hospital. Barely able to move or speak, the teacher, ninety at the time, motioned Crenshaw to bring his putter over to the bedside and proceeded to give his star pupil one last lesson, leaving him with his famous mantra: "Take dead aim."

For the four rounds of the Masters, it was as if Penick was walking beside Crenshaw, guiding his every shot. The last putting lesson he gave may have been his greatest. On the dastardly undulating greens of Augusta National Golf Club that roll at the speed of polished titanium, Crenshaw, in the twilight of his PGA Tour career, did not have a single three-putt the entire week.

Matthew Harris remembers the setting well, including the moment Crenshaw broke down with bittersweet joy. The whole thing served not as the quintessential moment of the tournament but more as an exclamation to the entire emotion-fueled week. Indeed, Matthew had his own unforgettable experience at Augusta that year.

A well-known golf photographer, Matthew, then thirty-four, journeyed to the Augusta course to shoot the Masters for the German *Golf Journal* with the knowledge that his father, Derek Harris, sixty-six, was seriously ill, though by no means on his deathbed.

On the Friday of tournament week, Matthew made his way to the tee of the 6th hole, a little-known spot even for other photographers, and one of his favorite locations on the course because of its panoramic view of both the 6th and 16th greens. He recalls the day vividly.

"The flowers that year were particularly strong and bold in color," he says. "Where I was, the azaleas were all in full bloom. I cannot explain why, but something struck me to look down and I saw one pod, which had flowered, had fallen off, and was lying on the ground. There was nothing else."

As Matthew bent to retrieve the flower, he was enveloped by what he calls an "aura."

"I just knew instantly as I picked it up that my dad had died."

There was no fear or panic or sadness that came with the realization, but an uncanny calm.

"I suppose when I snapped out of that aura, I just went about my job," proceeding to take photos for the rest of the day, realizing that there was nothing he could do to bring comfort to his mother that his brother and sister back in England weren't already doing.

That evening, about a half hour after Matthew returned to the home where he was staying for the tournament, the phone rang. On the other end was his mother.

"Don't worry; I know Dad's died," Matthew said to his mother. He told her about the events on the Augusta course while she listened in stunned silence.

"I can't believe what you've told me" was all Matthew's mother could muster when she was finally able to speak again.

Matthew decided to remain at the tournament, telling only one close friend of his father's passing. As the tournament moved on and it was now obvious Crenshaw was writing a remarkable story, it heightened the intensity of what the photographer was enduring.

"There wasn't just a lot of emotion in me, there was also a lot of emotion in that tournament."

On Saturday he stayed away from the 6th hole, but on Sunday he was drawn back to the special location late in the day as Crenshaw was making his charge to the title. Matthew made the long uphill walk along the 17th and 18th holes over to the 6th and up to the tee.

"I did it because I was drawn to it, not because I made some dramatic artistic decision," he says.

When he arrived, Harris was amazed at what lay before him. The azaleas were still in bloom and the picturesque scene of the 16th green was enhanced by the spreading afternoon shadows. Harris put the camera to his eye and clicked away as Crenshaw was making the birdie that all but secured the stunning victory, sending a thunderous roar of approval from the crowd over the hallowed course as the putt dropped.

"The view I got was beautiful. You know it's the 16th. You know it's Crenshaw."

It was then that Matthew had his second encounter at the Masters. Standing alone on the tee, with no one within hundreds of yards of him, his senses were overtaken. "I could smell my father. It wasn't just the smell of the cigars, which he smoked, but there was something else with it," he says, at a loss to explain exactly what that was. "It's the person, isn't it?"

He looked around to be sure he was alone—even though he knew he was—with his father. After the smell dissipated, he made his way back toward the clubhouse in time to capture the incredibly emotional moment on the 18th green.

Matthew did not return to the 6th tee again until 2008, thirteen years after his father had died. To this day he considers himself lucky to have experienced what he did.

"It was a wonderful way to lose your father. I'm certainly at one with it," he says. "It still brings a wry smile to my face."

He's never tried to rationalize what happened to him on that course, but he knows for certain they were not imagined events.

"I'm not a religious person at all," says Matthew. "But I do consider myself a spiritual person."

In trying to explain the magical moments of the tournament, the words Crenshaw spoke about his victory could just as easily have been spoken by Matthew.

"So many times at Augusta you feel blessed," Crenshaw said. "I felt that way this week."

Lorne Rubenstein grew up just north of Toronto playing public golf courses. So he easily recalls the first time he found himself teeing up at a private facility. It was Maple Downs Golf and Country Club in nearby Richmond Hill, Ontario. Rubenstein's father, Percy, who ran an auto parts business, had been invited to play in a tournament at Maple Downs, so when one of the foursome backed out Rubenstein, barely fourteen at the time, was given the chance to play.

Fast forward to 1989. By then Lorne, forty, was a successful golf writer when his father died of a heart attack unexpectedly in May at the age of sixty-six.

Later that year Lorne found himself back at Maple Downs. As Lorne stood on the 10th tee, his father was the furthest thing from his mind. He was concentrating on the task at hand. The hole is a long par 4 with a drive up and over a hill. There is out-of-bounds on the right, which is where Pardes Shalom Jewish Cemetery sits. A right-hander, Lorne had a wicked right-to-left hook. On that day, though, as he laced his drive, it inexplicably sliced, flying right and more right, coming to rest in the cemetery where, it suddenly occurred to Lorne, his father was buried. He watched in surprise as the ball landed and bounded away, thinking to himself, "Oh my God, it's going to roll down to my father's grave."

As is custom, each synagogue has its own section, and Lorne's shot found its way down to the area reserved for Adath Israel, where his father is interred. Now a member of Maple Downs, Lorne says he has never again hit another tee shot into the cemetery.

Chapter 15

The Minikahda Club: Voices from a Murderous Past

In the scenic wonder of Minnesota sits Minikahda, one of the country's finest courses and the site of some legendary match play. It's also the scene of one of the state's most grisly murders and a place where ghosts regularly make their presence known. So thick are the spirits here that even golf's finest players can't help but be driven a bit mad.

The security guard shone his light into the dark corners of the empty clubhouse and held his breath. He followed the noise into the most remote part of the place. The massive old wooden building groaned and creaked as the wind off Lake Calhoun pushed at its sides.

Still, there was that other noise. The sound of voices was there, barely audible. The murmur and chatter rose and fell and seemed to be coming from everywhere and nowhere all at once.

"Who's in there?"

No reply. The sound rose to a crescendo, then abruptly stopped. The old Minikahda Club was left in grave-like silence. The guard backed out of the room and beat a hasty retreat to his desk. It was there the following morning his boss found him, pale and shaken.

"Steve, what in the world is wrong?" the manager asked.

"It was a pretty active night," the guard said cryptically.

"Active?"

"Jimmy, I got scared last night," said Steve, a strapping, no-nonsense retired cop who stood six-foot-four and weighed nearly 325 pounds. "I don't know whether it was the rats or the ghosts."

Jimmy knew Steve was a careful guy. Very alert and never prone to scaring easily.

"The clubhouse sure can be kind of creepy at night. But you know the old place was empty, right?" Jimmy said, trying to comfort his shaken employee.

"Jimmy, I'm not sure I was alone," Steve replied.

The guard told his coworker about the voices, how they seemed to be just out of range, perhaps around the next corner, or up the next stairway. He recounted how he'd followed the sound throughout the Minikahda Club. Just before they'd disappeared, he'd gotten the strange, terrific sensation that the voices were coming from beneath his feet.

"Was it someone in the function hall?" Jimmy asked. "Maybe somebody left behind after the wedding reception there?"

"No, Jimmy," Steve answered dryly. "It was the people between the floorboards."

The Minikahda Club is one of the grand old clubs of American golf, founded in the late 1890s when Minneapolis was at the western edge of the game's expansion across the United States. It remains a fantastic place to enjoy golf, tennis, a fine meal, or a relaxing drink on the porch of the understated clubhouse that looks out first over Lake Calhoun, then the downtown skyline.

Golf first arrived at Minikahda in the form of a nine-hole course that was later doubled to a full eighteen holes. When it was apparent the game was being played in earnest, famed architect Donald Ross was brought in to create an entirely new layout, considered among the finest in the country. Minikahda would host the biggest national events, including the U.S. Amateur and U.S. Open, as well as prominent regional and local tournaments. It remains to this day among the elite midwestern golf clubs.

As Steve the security guard and many others have discovered since, however, Minikahda has an odd and eerie thread of history running through it. And it has its share of ghosts. The trouble may have begun with Minikahda's very location. The site was chosen in the fall of 1895 after a group of picnickers—a group that included one of the club's founders—bicycled to the spot and fell in love with its scenic beauty. They dubbed the place "minikahda," the Sioux word for "place by the water." As they ate and relaxed by the lake that afternoon, the party was blissfully unaware that they were sitting just a few yards from the scene of one of Minneapolis's grisliest murders.

Less than a year before, in December 1894, a privileged ne'er-do-well named Harry Hayward lured dressmaker Catherine "Kitty" Ging into a horse-drawn carriage on the pretense of attending the opera. The two were friends and Kitty, though engaged to another man at the time, had a deep infatuation for Harry. The son of a wealthy real-estate developer, he was a dapper, handsome man who was also an incorrigible gambler with ties to petty criminals and counterfeiters. Not long before her death,

Harry had taken out two $5,000 life insurance policies on Kitty.

The gambling con man was unable to commit the horrendous crime on his own. Harry convinced a janitor in Kitty's apartment building, the posh Ozark Flats, to murder the woman for $2,000. After initially agreeing, Claus Blixt tried to back out of the despicable deal, but Harry threatened to harm the man's family. That fateful night, Claus Blixt put a bullet in the back of Kitty's head and dumped her body along the shore of Lake Calhoun. At the exact moment her corpse was being discovered in the woody swamp, a horse pulling an empty buggy, its cushions dripping with blood, trotted into Gossman's Livery Stable. Kitty had rented the vehicle there earlier in the evening.

Within three days, plotter and killer were arrested after Harry's brother Adry turned them in.

In a newspaper photo montage of the actors in the grisly drama, Claus, referred to as "The Assassin," looks out with a sort of boyish confusion. He spent the rest of his life behind bars as the result of his crime. Harry is pictured in a dark suit, white shirt, and white silk tie, the very same outfit he wore to his hanging.

A year and seven days after the murder, the trapdoor of the gallows swung open, Harry Hayward's body dropped, the rope tightened, his necked snapped, and his life ended. He displayed dark humor, cynicism, and no remorse right to the end. According to one newspaper account, just moments away from death, the condemned man yelled to a group of gawkers standing below the gallows pole.

"When Harry Hayward is hung, his ghost will turn around and say that it is ashamed of his body," Harry shouted.

Even as the noose was about to be placed on his head, his bravado remained. His last words were: "Keep up your courage, boys, pull her tight; I stand pat. Goodbye."

Such morbid history in and around the old club has clearly had an influence on events there, which range from subtle supernatural influences to downright terrifying events. In the category of the former, Minikahda was the stage for one of the strangest matches in amateur golf history, in which two pillars of the great game came to detest each other, one acting so out of character it was, those who witnessed it say, as if he were possessed by a demon.

Three years before the great Bobby Jones came to Minnesota to take the third leg of the 1930 Grand Slam at Interlachen Country Club, he developed a great fondness for the area. It was at Minikahda in 1927 that Jones won the third of his four U.S. Amateur titles, all within a five-year period.

Jones was a medalist in the qualifying round that year with a total of 142. He made his way through match play and in the finals bested the Midwest's best player, Charles "Chick" Evans, in what was originally scheduled to be a thirty-six-hole showdown. In 1916 Evans had won the U.S. Amateur and the U.S. Open, held at Minikahda, becoming the first to win both tournaments in the same year. In 1927 he was given a good chance to beat the best player ever, even though he was much older.

The conclusion of that U.S. Amateur in 1927 was by far the oddest ending to any tournament in which Jones participated. It was one of the only times in a national tournament that Jones showed the anger he was famous for in private but almost never displayed during competition.

According to the official version, the match ended on the 29th hole when Evans leaned over to line up his putt and inadvertently moved the ball, costing him the hole, the match, and the championship. The honorable Evans called the penalty on himself, so the account goes. He immediately stood and conceded defeat. He walked over to Jones and shook his adversary's hand, signaling that the inevitable had arrived. At least that's how the papers portrayed it, and how the story was told for more than thirty-six years. Evans and Jones were considered not only great golfers, but also two of the finest gentlemen in the game; there was no reason to doubt the "official" account.

Then in 1963, Evans, by then in his late seventies, told a different story to the Associated Press, one that served to deflate a significant part of the Jones legend.

The day of the final at Minikahda, according to Evans, Jones showed a surprising, uncharacteristic anger as soon as the first golf balls were launched. "It wasn't the beating so much as the way it was done," Evans said. "On the first tee, Jones told me I had teed my ball in front of the markers. Later he called me for putting my finger into the grass."

The disagreements would culminate as the two played the 11th green for the second time that day.

"On what became the last hole of our match, I putted to within two inches of the hole. I thought he might concede the two-inch putt. I looked at him and he just stood there, about a yard from me, staring at me. I went up to my ball, and when I put my putter head down, it touched the ball," Evans said. "I looked up at Jones. 'The ball didn't move,' I said. 'It sure did,' Jones replied."

Evans decided not to argue and sarcastically congratulated Jones.

When told of the account, Jones refuted the story vehemently. In a letter to a friend, he wrote that Evans "preferred being the apparent victim of a misfortune to playing the long 12th hole up the hill away from the clubhouse."

Nonetheless, the criticism from Evans had to have hurt Jones. In the first two decades of the twentieth century, Evans was America's finest player. Along with the 1916 Amateur and Open, he captured the amateur again in 1920. Later he formed the Evans Scholarship, which has helped over eight thousand caddies attend college. Ironically, in 1960 Evans won the Bob Jones Award, the highest honor bestowed by the USGA.

If that match was one of the strangest on-course occurrences, for years there have been reports of odd happenings in and around the clubhouse at Minikahda, as well as reports of strange sounds in a former building taken down in the 1990s. Perhaps it is the ghost of Kitty Ging or the spirits of the long-dead murderers Harry Hayward and Claus Blixt returning to the scene of their heinous crime. Perhaps Jones and Evans are back to renew the feud. Or it might be, as some contend, the spirits of Native Americans who lived around the lake centuries before golf was ever played there.

No matter the cause, Jimmy Bennek says there definitely are ghosts at Minikahda. Jimmy has spent nearly fifty years working for the club, the past forty or so as the starter. As such, he's come to know nearly every living member and employee, past or present, as well as their stories. While he's never had any experience with noises or the entities that are said to inhabit the various buildings on the property, he is intimately familiar with the tales of those who have.

Many, like the security guard, Steve, encountered unexplained phenomena but never saw the spirits that dwell within the historic old club. Others, however, have certainly laid eyes on the otherworldly beings that haunt Minikahda.

One former locker room attendant, an old man we'll call Bert, worked at Minikahda from the 1930s into the 1960s, but his retirement didn't keep him from the club. He'd stop into the clubhouse on occasion and eventually struck up a friendship with Jimmy Bennek.

"You know, if you come into the place early, you might have a visitor," Bert told Jimmy. The old man never let on exactly what he'd seen in his years at the place, though he indicated he'd seen quite a bit.

"Bert was firmly convinced that something was in that building," Jimmy says.

And Bert was not alone in that opinion. Workers often tell the story about the building east of the clubhouse facing Lake Calhoun that was once used for employee housing. The rooms were small, just six by eight feet, with warped walls and badly sloping ceilings.

"It was kind of a peaceful place," Jimmy says as if trying to find some redeeming quality in the old dorm. The last person to reside there was an assistant golf pro who had the quarters to himself for a year and a half.

"He wasn't all that crazy about staying there," Jimmy recalls. "He said the building groaned a little every now and then."

The pro was also convinced there was some physical connection between the dorm and clubhouse, some sort of hidden tunnel or passageway. There isn't, of course, but "he had it in his mind there were goings-on back and forth between the buildings," Jimmy says, adding, "It might have been the fifty-pound raccoons we have around here."

Jimmy has no ghost stories of his own, so he likes to recount one he's made up. When the wind comes in off Lake Calhoun in just a certain way, it starts the white wicker chairs on the side porch of the clubhouse to rocking. Jimmy tells visitors that the movements are the result of ghosts of long-gone members, deceased relatives, or one of the more famous players who have shot their last round at Minikahda and gone on to a better place.

"That must be Harry," Jimmy will say, nodding toward the chair, remembering the fine amateur Harry Legg, who called Minikahda his home course.

But while he's making up his own ghostly tales, Jimmy harbors not even the slightest doubt that what Bert, Steve, and countless others have told him is the truth. He knows there are ghosts and spirits at Minikahda.

"Knowing these people they way I know these people, they called a spade a spade," Jimmy concludes.

Chapter 16

Lincoln Park Golf Course: Walking Atop the Dead

It may be beautiful on the surface, but beneath the manicured turf of the Lincoln Park Golf Course lies a scene as macabre as any ever witnessed. Thousands of corpses remain barely covered by the fairway grass. If you're dining in the area, just don't order the ribs.

It is hard to imagine there are many municipal golf courses anywhere in the world more scenic than the one on the north side of San Francisco. The facility sits high on a bluff, offering a stunning view of the bay and the famed Golden Gate Bridge. The idyllic Lincoln Park Golf Course has hosted players since 1902, when three holes were laid out and residents of the city were allowed to tee up for free, a tradition that continued for decades.

In 1909, three years after the San Francisco earthquake, as golf's popularity was increasing, six more holes were added, giving the city its first nine-hole layout. The course would become ten holes, and later fourteen and finally eighteen holes in 1917, when architect Tom Bendelow was brought in to create an entirely new design. The par-68 course is 5,149 yards long and forested with mature cypress and pine trees along with lots of native landscaping. Most of the course features rolling hills, though in more than a few places golfers are required to trek up and down the kinds of steep hills the city by the bay is so famous for. The picturesque Lincoln Park is one of the courses used for the annual San Francisco City Golf Championships.

As peaceful as the spot may be, however, what lies beneath the turf is enough to knock even the most relaxed golfer off his game. The grim reality of the course might also harbor a clue to the unexplained noises and mysterious happenings in the clubhouse, incidents that frightened one group of workers so badly they refused to work in the place after dark.

Below the rolling fairways, tees, and greens lay thousands of corpses, some say as many as fifteen thousand, interred during the four decades the site served as a cemetery, making Lincoln Park golf's version of the horror movie *Poltergeist*. Newspaper stories from the early 1920s say the coffins and grave markers were moved from Lincoln Park to a new cemetery in the nearby town of Colma, a place created in 1924 for the specific purpose of burying San Francisco's dead. Colma, which still is the final resting place for thousands every year, is unofficially known as the City of the Silent. In a place where the dead greatly outnumber the living, the town's unofficial motto remains: "It's great to be alive in Colma."

"I got some news for you," says Lincoln Park general manager Lance Wong with a chuckle. "The tombstones may have been moved, but the bodies have not."

The first clue for golfers that they had been playing on top of the dead did not come until the mid 1990s, when the California Palace of the Legion of Honor museum was being retrofitted to better withstand earthquakes. The building opened in 1923 on property that abuts the golf course; its original construction facilitated the rerouting of the golf course.

During excavation of the courtyard, construction workers unearthed hundreds of coffins. Wiley Holman, the owner of the cultural resource consulting firm of Holman and Associates, was in charge of archaeology on the site and estimates that eight hundred graves were dug up before the project was shut down by the museum's directors. Because the wooden markers had been removed more than eighty-five years earlier, and the city's death records had been destroyed in the fires resulting from the 1906 San Francisco earthquake, only two of the corpses could be identified. Both were the bodies of Chinese immigrants, which came as a shock to investigators. While the cemetery was in use, it was a violation of city ordinance to bury a Chinese national within San Francisco's city limits. Usually when one of the city's many Chinese immigrants died, the body or ashes were stored until enough money could be raised to have the remains sent back to China.

A mausoleum Wong says was used as a temporary home for the ashes of cremated Chinese immigrants remains on the course.

For the Chinese bodies that were buried, tradition called for placing a brick with Chinese writing facedown on the coffin before it was covered with dirt. The brick could be used to identify the deceased if the grave was disturbed.

In the two coffins Wiley and his workers unearthed that held Chinese remains, one contained an elderly woman who was buried with her opium pipe and other traditional items. She had a piece of jade in her mouth, another common Chinese custom of the time. The second coffin held a small child along with two kidney-shaped glass bottles containing a white liquid, perhaps milk.

The discovery set off an inquiry into just what was beneath the surface of Lincoln Park. As it turns out, the place was originally known as City Cemetery. It was first used as a pauper's field for the homeless and the poorest residents but was later expanded to include non-indigents as well. Eventually the cemetery was sectioned off by ethnicity with areas for Mexicans, Greeks, and African Americans, among others. The part under the Legion of Honor was thought to be predominantly French, at least until the surprise discovery of the Chinese woman and child.

Many of the skeletons Wiley unearthed recounted, in their own way, the difficult and dangerous life residents of San Francisco faced in the 1800s. Some were without legs, many had multiple broken bones, and one was found with the bullet that killed him still lodged in his rib cage. Some of the corpses beneath the adjacent Legion of Honor property had been protected from the elements and were thus so well preserved that skin was still on the bones.

Also found were boxes containing animal and human carcasses that were dissected by students of a nearby medical school. Some of the unfortunate critters had been partially preserved with rudimentary embalming methods. Wiley said the stench that came from those containers in particular was among the most vile he has ever encountered in his career of opening coffins. It was bad enough to make some of his seasoned employees leave the job site, never to return. Wiley describes the foul mass of decaying flesh inside these coffins as "ookie," which he swears is a technical term.

It wasn't just Wiley's workers who were grossed out by the macabre find. One area of morbid excavation took place right up against one of Lincoln Park's tee boxes. A plastic privacy fence was erected to keep golfers from witnessing the grotesque endeavor. But not all of the golfers could resist the temptation to have a peek over the barrier. Wiley says he was most impressed by the fortitude of one inebriated, early-morning foursome in particular.

"They were already three sheets to the wind when they got there. They asked us what we were doing, looked over the fence and threw up, then kept going," Wiley says, laughing at the recollection.

Wiley's digging in the courtyard of the Legion of Honor, built in tribute to all the soldiers who fought in World War I, uncovered another surprise—an empty underground mausoleum for two, apparently constructed for sugar magnate Adolph B. Spreckels and his wife, museum founder Alma de Bretteville Spreckels, known as "Big Alma" and the "Great-Grandmother of San Francisco."

Officials of the Legion of Honor halted the project and confiscated Wiley's records. They told Wiley the unearthed coffins have since been reburied at a secret location outside the city limits. But that's far from the greatest indignity the dead have suffered around Lincoln Park.

Wiley said during the coffin recovery, it was discovered that some of the original foundations on the property run right through coffins and the bodies inside them. Wiley likes to point out that the legion's cafeteria, for example, is below ground level, meaning diners are unaware they are enjoying their meals just a few feet from dozens of hideously severed human remains.

"I just tell people not to order the ribs," Wiley says with a bit of an evil laugh.

Wong and others who have spent a fair amount of time around Lincoln Park were not completely shocked by the morbid discovery beneath the links. For years golf maintenance workers have been unearthing shards of bone whenever they dig more than a few inches below the turf for such jobs as installing irrigation heads. Groundhogs tunneling on the property also frequently kick up remains of San Francisco's dead.

Most believe that the spirits that inhabit the clubhouse, which opened in 1922, are connected to the graves.

Wong said haunted encounters at Lincoln Park always occurred after sunset and were so frequent and scary that, at one point, the company cleaning the clubhouse refused to go into the place at night when it was empty.

"They would only clean during the day because there were no spirits then," he says.

Wong said the most repeated experience was that of workers hearing noises that sounded like a party or a loud television coming from a closed-off room. Usually security or maintenance personnel working late at night would hear the racket and assume that some miscreants had gotten into someplace they should not be and were making a mess or worse. When the door was opened, however, the sound would stop immediately and the room would invariably be empty.

If Wong had his doubts about the stories, they were erased late one night following a municipal election. The clubhouse was used as a polling station and Wong was cleaning up after everyone had gone home, or so he thought. From inside one of the function rooms he heard what sounded like multiple voices.

"Let me get these people out of here," he thought to himself. But when he pulled the door open, he found only a dark, empty, and deathly silent room.

"I didn't look to see what was going on; I just got the heck out of there," he says.

There was one former employee, a dishwasher, who was so scared by what happened in Lincoln Park's clubhouse that he would not even discuss the subject.

"He'd freak out every time we brought up ghosts," Wong says.

The dishwasher told coworkers what so rattled him was that on many occasions he would be standing over the sink doing his job when he would feel a tap on his shoulder. Turning around expecting to find a coworker, he instead found himself all alone. At the same moment when he found himself standing in an empty kitchen, the man would feel an icy chill envelop him.

Wong has no explanation for the strange events of the past. Moreover, he cannot explain why the haunting of Lincoln Park now seems to have ceased. There hasn't been a ghost sighting or a report of supernatural activity at Lincoln Park for nearly a decade. The ghosts may be gone for now, but the bodies, the thousands upon thousands of bodies, most assuredly remain.

Chapter 17

Mount Lawley Golf Club: Death on Satan's Elbow

Mount Lawley Golf Club boasts one of the finest courses in all of Australia. What the club histories won't tell you, however, is how a young man met a bitter death on a part of the links named for the devil himself. When teeing up at the Mount Lawley, if the stiff Perth winds don't rattle you, the ghost of a distraught young man just might.

The day started routinely enough for greens keeper James Elliot. It was a Monday morning late in the 1933 golf season, and the weather was unusually hot all around Perth, Australia. James decided to make quick rounds of the Mount Lawley Golf Club before the sun got too high.

As James trundled down the 11th fairway, he spied something large lying on the green. As he moved closer, he saw it was a well-dressed young man, prostrate between the fringe and the pin.

The idea that some miscreant would get drunk enough to wander onto his course and have a nap on his greens infuriated the old man.

"Hey there, you! Get up!" James shouted. "Get up. You'll damage the grass. This is private property!"

There was no response. James quickened his step to a trot. He came up to the man, who was lying on his side, facing away from him. When he reached down to the man's shoulder, he found it cold and stiff. He rolled the man toward him and made a gruesome discovery. Eyes agape, skin gone white and cold, lips blue and covered with a bloody froth. Death had come to the Mount Lawley. Next to the body, a strange-looking bottle lay empty on the grass. The old man ran back to the clubhouse to call the police.

In short order, the course was crawling with investigators.

"Who is he?" James asked one of the detectives, a cop named Jim Stacey.

"His name's Michael," Stacey said. "Don't know much more than that right now."

"Did he die of the drink?" James Elliot asked.

"My guess is it was something far worse than that," the cop answered as he poked at the curious-looking bottle with his pencil. He wrote something in his notepad, then scanned the length of the fairway.

"What is this, the 10th hole?" Jim Stacey asked the greens keeper. "11th?"

"Clootie's," the old man replied.

"Excuse me?"

"Clootie's. Clootie's Elbow," James Elliot said. "Like in Scotland, we call the holes by their names here, not their numbers. This is Clootie's Elbow."

"And what does Clootie mean?" the cop asked.

"Satan."

The mysterious death of a young man was not the kind of thing that happened at the Mount Lawley, one of Australia's finer private clubs in an affluent suburb north of Perth. The club had been growing over the previous two years as an enthusiastic membership pumped money and resources into the development of the place. Members from the wealthiest families in the region were known to roll up their well-pressed sleeves to cut brush, rake sod, and dig bunkers in pursuit of their dream of a championship club of their own.

By 1929, four years before James Elliot came upon Michael's body, the eighteen-hole Australian course designed by well-known Royal Perth professional David Anderson was already garnering national acclaim as the best course in western Australia. The 6,795-yard, par-72 course features tight, tree-lined fairways, more than sixty bunkers, green-side traps cut close to the putting surfaces, and firm, slick greens. True to its name, Clootie's Elbow really is a devil of a hole; it's by far the toughest on the course. The 447-yard par-4 requires a strong drive to the corner to leave a direct shot to the pin. Anything less leaves a blind shot to a severely sloping green that makes any putt outside of two feet a test of nerves, with or without ghosts and spirits.

Reminiscent of the more famous sandbelt courses in Melbourne, the Mount Lawley's signature hole is its 13th, called Commonwealth. The hole is a short, downhill par-3 with a green in the shape of Australia herself and a fairway that sits wide open in the treacherous western Australian winds. Atop the pin flies, of course, a miniature Aussie national flag. Commonwealth is played from an elevated tee into the prevailing easterly sea breezes. Pin placements and greens locations are described by locals according to where they fall on the Aussie map. Alice Springs always represents a safe target, especially when the pin is cut at Kalgoorlie or Broken Hill, the Mount Lawley regulars will gladly attest.

Other highlights, in addition to Commonwealth and Clootie's—or Satan's—Elbow, include a dogleg right 12th hole, appropriately dubbed Boomerang, and a deceptively short 300-yard par-4 16th called the Trap. The name comes not from a particular course feature, but from the temptation to hit over a stand of trees to the green. Failure is invariably costly.

Other colorful names that take the place of numbered holes on the Mount Lawley layout include: Pumphouse, Paperbark, the Roadway, and Bunker Hill. The names add a certain quirkiness to the sandy track in the Perth suburbs.

It's not that the place didn't have its share of oddities from the outset. When the course first opened in 1929, getting water to all parts of the extremely dry fairways remained difficult. A foul-smelling scum clogged the irrigation heads and the grass grew in weak and scrubby. Large patches of sand and dirt left golf balls the same color as the ground, making them nearly impossible to find. Ever resourceful, the early Mount Lawley regulars took to using bright red balls. The practice was short-lived, however, as players found even the most perfectly struck drives disappearing from the fairway. The local crows mistook the red balls for berries and absconded with them for what was likely a disappointing snack.

Conditions continued to improve over the years and in 1956, Mount Lawley got its first national attention when it hosted both the Australian State Open and Amateur Championships. Gary Player took the Open and Len Thomas won the Amateur. Changes were made to the layout, including the narrowing of some fairways, to help the club achieve championship status. The understated clubhouse at Mount Lawley was positioned to provide some spectacular views over the club's tranquil undulating fairways, most of which are surrounded by forbidding, heavily wooded roughs. By

1956 the entrance to the Mount Lawley was, as it is today, through a gate in an impressive Toodyay stone wall that speaks to the exclusivity of the club and the affluence of its members. It is the home course of many of Perth's richest and most powerful business and political leaders.

But in 1930 the ambulance that carried the quickly stiffening body of an otherwise strapping young man off the course made its way in and out of a rickety wire dairy fence that secured the club's main driveway off Walter Road.

At the morgue the coroner found that both the victim's stomach and the strange-looking bottle contained a powerful cocktail of poisons, including strychnine. Subsequent inquiry by the Perth City Court determined that the young man had died from ingesting the poison. In the ensuing years, many urban legends have grown up around Michael's death. In some versions his last name is Oakley or Oakleigh, an Irish immigrant lured to the course by thugs who robbed and tortured him before forcing him to drink the poison that killed him. The official verdict in the matter, however, is that the man found dead that morning in 1933, his heart heavy because of some family turmoil, wandered alone onto the Mount Lawley golf course, sat down on the green at Satan's Elbow, and drank the poison that killed him. His painful death throes may have lasted thirty to forty agonizing minutes. He expired several hours before he was discovered stretched out unceremoniously on the Clootie's putting surface.

The memory of Michael's suicide might well have died with him in the waning warmth of the 1933 golf season. Club members have always been reluctant to discuss the matter. Several area newspapers covered the death and subsequent investigation on their front pages, but all have since redacted the victim's last name in their archives per Australian press rules governing the coverage of suicides. Though the very public suicide is often blamed for a fairly steep corresponding drop in membership in the early 1930s, and despite the fact that it is among the most notable events at the place, the grisly affair gets no mention in any official Mount Lawley club history.

But the dead man himself was apparently unsatisfied with simply fading away into western Australia's forgotten past.

In the past seventy-five years, there have been countless reports of supernatural experiences everywhere on the Mount Lawley course, but especially around the hole the locals call Clootie's Elbow. Witnesses say the encounters range from a general feeling of terror, to unexplained glowing orbs and auras, to actual ghost sightings. In the world of ghosts and ghost hunting, it's not unusual for folks to report supernatural experiences in places where the odd unusual or unattended death has occurred. Most interesting to paranormal investigators about Mount Lawley, however, is the number of reports of terrifying encounters coming from people who had never heard of the ghastly suicide seven decades ago.

One woman, a seasoned paranormal investigator who visited the club after reading a growing list of ghostly accounts posted on the Internet, told associates she was absolutely horrified by her experience at Mount Lawley. She declared the place among the most haunted in western Australia and "certainly the most haunted golf course I've ever encountered."

Other guests have seen the floating lights and orbs rolling along Mount Lawley's fairways, especially in the area close to the 11th hole, where both the devil and a young man named Michael maintain a history intertwined with the club. A few witnesses, some who have never heard the tale of the 1933 suicide, claim to have seen a sad-looking chap dressed in an Aussie army uniform with a felt "slouch" hat moping around the fringes of the course. A photo of the suicide victim named Michael dressed in such a uniform was published with his obituary in the Perth area newspapers in 1933.

The ghost never confronts anyone, just makes his way silently along the edge of the woods as if looking for a place to be alone. If followed, the apparition simply vanishes without a sound, eyewitnesses claim.

If a ghost really does roam Satan's Elbow or any other part of the golf course, however, the Mount Lawley regulars are keeping it to themselves. One employee, who would identify himself only as Justin, says the rumors of ghosts are not something anyone at Mount Lawley cares to discuss. Has he heard of the strange suicide of a young man on the second hole there in 1933? No comment there either.

"Don't you care to talk about golf?" Justin asks, clearly annoyed.

Indeed there is plenty of great golf to talk about at Mount Lawley. But for those who dare venture there, keep in mind there may be more lurking in the thickets that border the rough, things you won't hear about from the folks in the clubhouse or read about anywhere in the Mount Lawley brochure.

Chapter 18

Snow Hill Country Club: A Room with a Boo

Snow Hill puts the "country" in country club with a terrific rural course devoid of townhouses and condos. And the six luxury rooms in the inn above the clubhouse make the place a perfect spot to get away from it all. Unless, of course, it's ghosts you're trying to get away from. At Snow Hill the spirits are part of the attraction.

The Harris family had a secret.

On the surface all was tranquil around their property in Clinton County, Ohio. But deep beneath the stately white-washed Federal brick building where Charles Harris and his wife, Catherine, made their home and their living, things were often anything but still. In a labyrinth of secret rooms and passageways, there was nearly constant movement. And fear.

Charles Harris was a "stationmaster." Almost since the day he'd built his home in 1806, the place had been a stop on the famous Underground Railroad, the famed informal network of boats, trains, wagons, and safe houses that helped more than thirty thousand escaped slaves flee the United States and reach freedom in Canada. Stationmasters like Charles offered up their homes to hide the runaway slaves. From Maine to Michigan, hundreds of abolitionists faced grave risk to themselves and their families in order to make good on their beliefs.

Even before he converted the cellar into a hiding place for escaped slaves, Charles and Catherine called their home

Snow Hill in memory of their beloved ancestral homes in Snow Hill, Maryland. Charles built his new family homestead in New Vienna, Ohio, on Route 73, between Hillsboro and Wilmington and due east of Cincinnati. When he turned the place into a tavern, and later a hotel in 1820, he also made sure Snow Hill remained an important waypoint in Ohio's copious collection of Underground Railroad stops. The effort was a noble one, though the actual operation of a "station" could be difficult and deadly. The arduous travel, which required secret passage for the escapees across thousands of miles of rural terrain, limited the Underground Railroad mostly to young, healthy blacks. Even so, sickness and death stalked the freedom seekers with the same tenacity as the southern bounty hunters. As Charles and his associates took in new freed slaves and notified their fellow Underground Railroad "conductors" and "agents" of the escapees' travel plans, he witnessed his share of former slaves sadly ending their life's journey in the dark holding areas and tunnels under his property. Thus began the rich history of the Snow Hill Inn and Country Club, a place of both comfort and misery, and lately a place of mystery.

Snow Hill surely has endured a great deal since the heyday of the Underground Railroad ended in 1850. In 1896 the place was auctioned off when Charles Harris's granddaughter Lucy died. For more than two decades it sat mostly vacant and fell into disrepair. It was Lucy's niece, Nancy Norma Crabbs, who brought the place back into the Harris fold when she and her husband bought Snow Hill in 1920. The couple renovated the inn, stuffing the rooms with quaint antiques and marketing it as a luxury retreat.

The Crabbs built a nine-hole golf course adjacent to the inn in 1924. The first attempt at golf was admirable if not remarkable. Don McNeil, Snow Hill's 1941 club champion, was just twelve years old when the club debuted and he served as a caddy for the first foursome to ever play Snow Hill. He once cracked that the original nine-holer "would have made for a better cornfield than a golf course." Still, the world-class greens earned a reputation that attracted several big-name players, including the legendary Walter Hagen. The two-time U.S. Open champ and the first American to win Britain's Open Championship found time to tee up at Snow Hill during his travels between his home course in Michigan and his childhood home in Rochester, New York.

The inn also began getting noticed for its blend of quaint country solitude and luxury. Snow Hill played host over the years to such luminaries as Eleanor Roosevelt and Henry Ford. When the Crabbs died childless in 1947, Snow Hill Country Club members purchased the property from the estate. Interested more in golf than hospitality, the inn was shut down. Club members used the first floor of the building as the clubhouse. The second-floor rooms were used mostly for storage or were kept locked. And so the place remained for the next five decades. The most significant change in that period came in 1991 when the club hired Cincinnati golf course developer Denny Acomb, designer of both Hickory Woods and Crooked Tree, to expand that forgettable nine-hole track to a full eighteen holes. The place fell on tough financial times, however. After a failed attempt in 2002 to attract new players by making Snow Hill semiprivate, the place slipped toward insolvency.

The club finally went bankrupt in November 2004. At a final party in the clubhouse, members ate, drank, and reminisced until midnight, when the power company turned off the electricity. They left the place in silence and darkness, with food and drink still on the tables and balloons still hanging from the rafters, according to media reports at the time.

Later that year Cincinnati businessman Robert Henderson purchased Snow Hill at auction and has set about refurbishing both the guest rooms and the course. Today the stately old inn has once again become a popular vacation retreat. The course, now under the management of Tartan Golf, now plays a deceptively short 6,449 yards, but the course is no cakewalk. The challenging 442-yard 4th hole features an uphill fairway with a creek running directly up its spine. It's as difficult a par-4 as anyone could want.

There is more to Snow Hill than great golf and a rich abolitionist history, however. The place is teeming with ghosts. For decades workers and guests have reported doors that open and close on their own, the smell of roses and women's perfume wafting through rooms long left unoccupied, and blasts of cold air rushing through Snow Hill's hallways on balmy evenings.

The ghostly activity can be particularly unnerving for Snow Hill's maids, who frequently discover rooms in total disarray minutes after they've been cleaned and tidied. Guests have seen and even photographed strange floating orbs of light that drift aimlessly through Snow Hill.

Paranormal investigators have combed through Snow Hill, trying to identify the source of the supernatural activity there. While just who is haunting the place remains a mystery, the spirits of Snow Hill do appear to be trying to tell the living who they are. Recordings made by professional ghost hunters Shelly Suitor and Kathy Powell of Dayton, Ohio, contain EVPs, or electronic voice phenomena, which the experts maintain is proof that something beyond the mortal realm is reaching out at Snow Hill. It's difficult to make out much of what the voices say on the tape, though some words and phrases are plainly audible. There are men's voices saying "hush" and "Please help me, Martha!" and a young girl calling, "Daddy."

Out on the golf course there stood for many years a phone at the 9th tee used primarily for ordering lunch. In 2004 the club stopped the service and cut the line but left the disconnected phone in place. According to several employees, that phone kept ringing throughout the 2004 golf season. When anyone dared answer, they heard, of course, nothing but a dead line. The ghosts evidently got the message by the end of the season. After the winter of 2004, the phone ceased ringing.

Hilary Osborne has been the banquet manager at Snow Hill for more than a decade. She says she didn't much believe in ghosts when she took the job, but the constant variety of encounters at the old inn has changed her mind.

"Within six months I started to notice strange things," says Hilary, who handles the steady stream of weddings, social occasions, and special events at Snow Hill. "Then one night two other employees and I saw a floating light that royally scared us. We couldn't explain it, and since then I've accepted that ghosts live at Snow Hill."

Hilary says she's also seen the banquet room's chandeliers spinning wildly and plates rattling in an empty kitchen.

Columbus native Chris Woodyard, author of *Ghost Hunters' Guide to Haunted Ohio* and the five-book *Haunted Ohio* series checked out the Snow Hill stories herself and left with the sense that the place is undeniably haunted.

"I saw a woman sitting in a chair draped in a blanket and she was cradling a child and crying," she told T. R. Massey, editor of the Ohio edition of *GolfStyles Magazine,* back in 2005. "It seemed like a snapshot, a video. I distinguish between a ghost that interacts with living beings and others that are just a snapshot or impression. She's a snapshot."

Woodyard also heard from a local cop who says he saw a ghostly woman in white in the same room.

After Henderson took over, Ty Day, a Tartan Golf employee, was brought to Snow Hill in 2005 to oversee the clubhouse rehab. Ty says he ordered huge trash containers placed around the property to help discard a century's worth of accumulated junk in the rooms on the building's second floor. His first inkling that something was amiss at Snow Hill came when workers started heaving the refuse out of the building. On most days workers would clean out rooms, then retire for the evening. They would return the next day only to find the stuff they'd trashed taken out of the trash bins and put back into the inn's storage rooms.

Ty also tried to protect one particular artifact at the club, but to no avail. Several times he took an old sepia-toned photo of a white-haired, bearded gent, one of Snow Hill's original members, from a locked trophy case in the club's restaurant. He put the fragile old picture in a drawer for safekeeping. Each time he did so, the photo made its way back into the trophy case.

Perhaps the oddest story at Snow Hill belongs to former golf manager David Stanton. David was on the club's second floor, poking around in what had been an old bathroom. The room still had the old porcelain fixtures, but the working plumbing had long since been removed. Despite that, David found the bathtub filled with crystal-clear water. He looked all around thinking the water might have come in through the roof but found no leaks anywhere. A bit spooked, David went to find someone to corroborate his discovery. When he returned with a fellow employee, the tub had been drained dry. Where the water had been, there was now only a coating of a mysterious fine grit that resembled fine sand or sugar.

Where some country clubs and hotels shy from their haunted nature, Snow Hill has decided to embrace it. They've renamed the bar the Spirits Bistro, and every fall weekend, guests are invited to take tours of the facility that are as informative as they are spooky. The tour groups go through the inn room by room examining the elegant bedrooms and parlors. They learn about Snow Hill's history and about life in the early 1800s. The group then heads into the basement and the old locker rooms for a true ghost hunt. Guests huddle in the dark where they can take pictures and ask questions of either the tour guides or the spirits that seem to abound in the historic building.

As part of the "Dinner and A Ghost" tour, the guests are treated to the recorded voices of the ghosts, something paranormal investigator Shelly Suitor says often wins over even the most jaded visitors.

"Many times guests arrive skeptical," Shelly says. "They think we're going to make stuff up, but they hear the tapes and their hearts start racing. Suddenly they're more open to the phenomena we see at Snow Hill."

In addition to the tapes, Snow Hill ghost tourists also get to witness a collection of ghostly videos and photographs taken at the inn. They are also equally likely to encounter a ghost on their own, Shelly says. During one tour through the former men's locker room, Shelly says, she and a group of guests clearly heard a man's voice tell her, "This is the men's room. Get out!"

The ghost tours have been so successful that Snow Hill recently added a "Sleep with A Ghost" package that combines the dinner and ghost tour, a little golf, and a room for the night for those still able to sleep after all the spooky tales and mysterious encounters.

Chapter 19

The Balsams Grand Resort Hotel: A Mountain of Mysteries

With unparalleled mountain and lake vistas, the Balsams Grand Resort is one of the premier golf destinations in the Northeast United States. But there is more to the place than its luxury hotel and outstanding courses. The old hotel has its share of ghosts bent on rattling the nerves of guests and employees alike.

"I just want to tell someone what happened. I know it sounds crazy. I just need to tell you this."

The woman on the phone took a deep, nervous breath. She'd called the manager's office at The Balsams Grand Resort Hotel, one of New Hampshire's most posh golf resorts, on a balmy June afternoon to tell a story from a much darker, much colder time.

"It happened four months ago," the woman began. "I . . . I couldn't talk about it until now."

One more deep breath and she began.

She and her husband were excited about their brief midwinter getaway to the northernmost reaches of New Hampshire. Tucked among the White Mountains along the Canadian border, the Balsams is far removed from the hustle of the city. On a frigid February night, the comfortable country chic of the resort's "new wing," built in 1918, can seem like the most romantically secluded place in the world. Or the most frightening.

After a day touring the nearby ski resorts, the couple had an early dinner. Afterward they ventured to the front porch and poked their heads out briefly into the biting cold and bitter winds enveloping the magnificent old hotel. They ducked back inside and retired to their cozy room for the evening. The woman was sound asleep just after midnight when a large thud startled her awake. Shaking off the confusion of sleep and the disorientation of being in a strange bed, the woman noticed that the bathroom light was still on, just as her husband had left it. Her eyes adjusted to the dimly lit room. That's when she saw him. Standing at the end of the bed, she saw a man looking toward the lighted bathroom.

"Are you all right, dear?" she called to the man, whom she assumed to be her husband. A familiar grunting response came from beneath the blankets to her left. Her husband was still tucked in snugly beside her.

"Who . . . ?"

The question died on her lips. She lay still, riveted in fear, looking at the shape of the strange man near the foot of the bed. She continued to stare at the figure of the man and watched in horrified amazement as he slowly, gradually disappeared right before her eyes.

"I know it sounds completely crazy," the woman told the hotel employee on the phone. The memory of the strange supernatural experience remained as fresh for her four months later as it had been in those few terrifying moments in the middle of that winter night.

And indeed, the woman's story might have sounded crazy to employees of the Balsams Grand Resort Hotel if they hadn't heard countless stories just like it. They might have dismissed it out of hand if many of them hadn't had their own supernatural experiences right there in the very same historic hotel. The Balsams is many things, including a vacationer's dream and a golfer's paradise. It is also undeniably haunted.

For nearly as long as people have been venturing to the quaint little town of Dixville Notch, New Hampshire, to take in the breathtaking scenery, the spectacular autumn colors, world-class skiing, and some of the Granite State's best resort golf, there have been spooky tales of the unexplained there. Ghostly apparitions, strange noises, mysterious writing, and playful pranks have become part of the ambience for visitors and staff alike at the Balsams.

Certainly the place has a rich enough history to have amassed an entire cadre of spirit dwellers bent on unnerving guests looking for a quiet golf getaway, or a romantic ski weekend. Any place that still refers to a section built in 1918 as "the new wing" has endured its share of blazing summers, frozen New England winters, and countless visitors, living and dead, roaming its halls. The ruffled sheer curtains and wrought iron fixtures that adorn each uniquely decorated room at the Balsams have seen their share of human drama over the past 150 years.

The Balsams Grand Resort Hotel traces its birth to the 1860s. In its earliest days, the Balsams welcomed its first guests as a twenty-five-room inn called the Dix House when it was opened and run by George Parsons. The place was named in honor of the town's founding father, Colonel Timothy Dix, a Revolutionary War hero and patriot who died in 1813 from injuries he sustained during the War of 1812. After Parsons's death, the hotel was taken over by his attorney and business partner, Daniel Webster, who at the time was on his way to becoming one of America's leading statesmen.

It was friends of Webster, the Whittemore family, who assumed the operation of the hotel. The Dix House became a well-known stop for travelers making their way along the Coos Trail and through the tiny town of Dixville Notch.

The hotel changed hands in 1895 when longtime guest and wealthy industrialist-inventor Henry S. Hale bought the Dix House. He renamed the place the Balsams and set about expanding and enhancing the property, with the final touch coming in 1918 with the completion of the Hampshire House, still known by regulars as "the new wing." Today the striking red-and-white Balsams Grand Resort Hotel, built in a combination of Spanish Renaissance and Rhenish styles sits on fifteen thousand acres and accommodates up to four hundred guests.

In addition to his ambitious expansion of the old hotel, Hale set about creating one of the jewels of New England golf at the Balsams. He'd been captivated by the famed Pinehurst Resort in Pinehurst Village, North Carolina, so much so that he began to refer to his own beloved Balsams as "the Summer Resort Pinehurst" in his advertisements. Hale felt strongly that the public's attraction to Pinehurst was due in large part to the magnificent championship golf course Donald Ross had designed for the southern resort. In 1897 Hale hired the Scotsman, who was residing in Massachusetts, to build his layout, now known as the Panorama course. True to its name, the Panorama offers stunning views of the surrounding White Mountains and Lake Gloriette, on which the hotel sits. There is also the executive nine-hole Coashaukee course, built several years later.

Visits to the Balsams aren't limited to the frivolity of golf, tennis, skiing, and the occasional New England wedding, however. The place also plays a role in one of the more quaint election traditions in the United States. Since 1952 New Hampshire has voted first in the presidential primaries, and in 1960 Dixville Notch was given the honor of being the first in the nation to turn in its results during the presidential election. The town is required to have every registered voter cast a ballot in order to hold onto its status. Every four years, just before midnight the day before the election, all the voters come to the Balsams for an official head count. The poll then opens at midnight as each of the voters casts his vote in the Ballot Room, all in about a minute. In 2008, seventeen votes were cast during the presidential primaries. In the first general election held in 1960, nine residents voted for Richard M. Nixon for president, and not a single vote was cast for John F. Kennedy, senator from the neighboring state of Massachusetts.

Snubbing JFK is far from the strangest thing that's ever occurred at the Balsams, however. From its scenic fairways, to its mountain vistas, to its lavish halls and plush guest rooms, the Balsams is a particularly haunted place. In most cases the ghosts at the Balsams show up just long enough to make their presence known and then disappear, leaving witnesses shaken and confused.

Late one night several years ago, an employee was headed to his own room on the top floor of the hotel after a long shift. Trudging wearily up the stairs, he suddenly stopped in his tracks. There, in a chair on the upper landing not far from his room, he saw a woman. The employee knew no other guests or workers should be in this part of the hotel at this late hour, but in a facility the size of the Balsams, folks are prone to wander.

Still, there was something about this woman that made the employee's blood turn cold. She sat perfectly still and quiet, but there was something distinctly out of place about her appearance. Her long, flowing ebony hair cascaded down her shoulders, where it all but disappeared against her long jet-black dress. It was a dress the worker could only describe as something from a bygone era. Her face was turned away from his, looking down the hallway as if waiting for someone else to arrive.

"Must be a guest who's gotten lost and stopped to rest," he thought to himself.

But as he approached the mysterious woman, the realization came over him in a terrifying wave. This was no guest. This was a ghost. He couldn't scream. Or move. He simply froze in place. Seconds later, when he had his wits about him again, he turned to beat a hasty retreat back down the stairs. As the frightened worker scurried away, he took one last look over his shoulder. The chair was empty. The ghostly woman in black had simply vanished.

The ghost sounds eerily similar to a vision that began, innocently enough, with a giggle. A young businessman staying at the Balsams was passing through the Dix social parlor one evening when he was enchanted by the sound of a woman's laughter. So seductive was the sound that he began to search the darkened room for her. He found nothing. Walking back to his room, the young man passed a large mirror in the stairway. In it he saw the reflection of a beautiful young woman in a long black dress. He was certain this was the woman he'd been looking for. When he turned to speak to her directly, however, he found himself alone in the hallway. Balsams employees have seen the ghostly woman moving through the lobby and walking down the third-floor halls of the Dix House as well.

The stories contain two recurring themes common to supernatural encounters at the Balsams: Witnesses often report a sudden realization that a human form they are looking at is actually a ghost. Many who have come face to face with the old hotel's spirits also say the apparitions quickly disappear once they've been seen by the living.

A decade ago a woman and her husband staying at the Balsams awoke in the middle of the night to find a man, naked and soaking wet, staring at them from the foot of their bed. As they continued to watch in horror, the man disappeared before their eyes. When they shared their story the next day, they were told that the man's description was an uncanny match for the hotel's former bandleader, who had drowned in Lake Gloriette nearly seventy years before. To their shock the couple were informed that they were staying in the very same room the bandleader lived in before his untimely demise.

One of the Balsams's longtime front-desk clerks has had a number of mysterious and unexplained encounters over the years. She's gotten accustomed to having her keys hidden. Finding them is almost always accompanied by the sound of giggling from the phantom prankster. And she's risen countless times to answer a knocking at her door, only to find the hallway empty.

Recently the desk clerk escorted one of her relatives into the Hale Room, one of the Balsams's impressive dining halls, named for the hotel's former owner. As they moved toward their table, the employee looked up to see a strange man standing by the fireplace. He beckoned her with one finger as if he recognized her.

"Excuse me for a moment," the clerk said to her companion. She set off across the room to see who this mysterious stranger was and what he wanted. Curious, her relative followed a few steps behind.

As she moved closer to him, it was clear this was no one she recognized. He was immaculately groomed, with a neatly trimmed moustache and, perhaps most curiously, he held a black formal top hat gingerly in one hand. It was at that moment she felt the same gripping sense of recognition her coworker had experienced at the top of the stairs years before. She knew in her rapidly beating heart she was looking at a ghost. The realization stopped her dead in her tracks.

"What? What's wrong?" the woman's companion asked.

"Him! Right there!" the desk clerk said, pointing at the apparition.

"I don't see anything," her relative said. "Just a shadow on the wall."

When the woman turned back from her companion to the ghost, he was gone. He'd vanished as quickly as he'd appeared.

Though she has never encountered him again, the desk clerk and several other employees have heard the clinking of silverware and spirited dinner conversation coming from an empty and dark Hale Room.

Perhaps the most unnerving ghost story at the Balsams involves one regular visitor who always got "special" treatment when lodging in his favorite room.

One morning after a steamy shower, the man found a message scrawled in red lipstick across the bathroom mirror.

"Ann, call Rita," the message read, along with an accompanying phone number.

When he first encountered it, the guest didn't think much of it. He assumed the maids had simply missed the lipstick smears during their rounds. He asked the staff to have the mirror cleaned, and they obliged.

A year later the man returned to the Balsams and asked to be put up in the same room. He spent an uneventful night there followed by a steaming-hot morning shower. Pulling back the shower curtains to grab a towel, the guest was shocked by what he saw. There in bright red lipstick written across the foggy mirror was the same message.

"Ann, call Rita."

Despite the creepy recurrence, the man insisted on staying in the same room every year for several years hence. He always found the same lipstick memo written on the mirror after his morning shower, something the staff, who had to clean the greasy missives, readily confirm. Oddly, no other guest ever encountered the messages on the mirror. When the man finally stopped coming to the Balsams, so too did the cryptic notes from Rita to Ann cease. Maybe Ann finally called Rita.

There are no particularly gruesome events in the Balsams's past to pin the hotel's supernatural activities on. Could Ann and Rita have been setting up a tee time? Perhaps the woman in black at the top of the stairs was a jilted lover eternally waiting for the return of some paramour.

And what of the mysterious mustachioed ghost by the fireplace? The description certainly bears a striking resemblance to the long-departed Henry S. Hale, the man who turned the Balsams into a place of world-class golf and grandeur. In the room that bears his name, it's easy to imagine him motioning an employee forward to point out an area that needs tending to, possibly looking to make sure his hotel is in perfect order.

Appendix:
For More Information

Victoria Golf Club
1110 Beach Drive
Victoria, BC V8S 2M9
Canada
(250) 598-4321
www.victoriagolf.com

Also:
Discover the Past Walking Tours
(800) 663-3883
www.discoverthepast.com

Trails West Golf Course
306 Cody Avenue
Fort Leavenworth, KS 66027
(913) 651-7176
www.legendsofamerica.com/OZ-FortLeavenworth.html

Mount Washington Hotel and Resort
Route 302
Bretton Woods, NH 03575
(800) 314-1752
www.mountwashingtonresort.com

Leatherstocking Golf Course
60 Lake Street
Cooperstown, NY 13326
(800) 348-6222
www.otesaga.com

Biltmore Hotel and Resort
1200 Anastasia Avenue
Coral Gables, FL 33134
(305) 913-3187
www.biltmorehotel.com

Also:
The Not So Tall Tale Tellers
(305) 274-1155
www.notsotalltaletellers.com

Ahwahnee and Wawona Hotels
P.O. Box 578
Yosemite National Park, CA 95389
(801) 559-4884
www.yosemitepark.com/Accommodations_TheAhwahnee
.aspx

Stafford Country Club
8873 Morganville Road (Route 237)
Stafford, NY 14143
(585) 343-9109

St. Andrews
West Sands Road
St. Andrews
Fife KY16 9XL
Scotland
44 (0) 1334 466666
www.standrews.org.uk/

Also:
www.saint-andrews.co.uk/History/martyrs.htm
www.exclassics.com/foxe/foxintro.htm
http://dlib.lib.ohio-state.edu/foxe/

Ladies' Golf Club of Toronto
7859 Yonge Street
Thornhill, ON L3T 2C4
Canada
(905) 889-3531
www.ladiesgolfclub.com

Greg Norman
501 North Highway A1A
Jupiter, FL 33477
(561) 743-8818
www.shark.com

Hilton Head
Golf Hilton Head Island
www.golf-hilton-head-island.com

Also:
www.seapines.com
www.seapinescountryclub.com
www.palmettohallgolf.com
www.longcoveclub.org

The Minikahda Club
3205 Excelsior Boulevard
Minneapolis, MN 55416
(612) 926-1601
www.minikahdaclub.org

Lincoln Park Golf Course
34th Avenue & Clement Street
San Francisco, CA 94121
(650) 759-3700
www.lincolnparkgc.com

Mount Lawley Golf Club
Walter Road
Inglewood, WA 6052
Australia
(618) 9271 9622
www.mlgc.org

Snow Hill Country Club
11093 SR 73
New Vienna, OH 45159
(937) 987-2491
www.snowhillcountryclub.com

The Balsams Grand Resort Hotel
1000 Cold Spring Road
Dixville Notch, NH 03576
(877) 225-7267
www.thebalsams.com

Acknowledgments

Special thanks go to Chris Hodenfield for the endorsement and the opportunity to work on this fascinating project.

Anthony Pioppi wishes to thank: my parents, Anne Guthrie, Nick and Stacey Chiocchio, Heather Garvin, Rick White, Eddie Adams, Dave and Lorraine Girard and the good people at Buoy One restaurant, Euan Grant, Dave "Tex" O'Brien, Ian Kinley, Wally Stolak at Hair of the Dog Saloon, Jim Dolan, Will Longo at Nikita's Bar and Bistro, Brian Silva, Peter Lessor at The Gatekeepers, Rob Lamy of Bridgestone Golf, Keith Angilly, Donnie Beck, Joe D'Ambrosio, Scott Ramsay, Stacey Viarengo, Brad Faxon, Sean Tully, Dave Silk, Tom DeGrandi, Ed Homsey, Bruce Berlet, Lisa Waddle, Fred Greene at Golf Smarter podcast, Gil Hanse, Brett Zimmerman, Cliff Drezek, Larry Aylward, Kyle Zimmerman, Geoffrey Childs, Tripp Davis, Noel Freeman, David Joy, Bumpy Chimes, Rick Dunfey, Lawson, Vicky and Rob Breault, Brad Klein, Rachel and Sean Donnelly, Tim Murphy, Irene Donnell, John Irvin and the staff at the Otesaga Resort Hotel and Leatherstocking Golf Course, Hunki Yun, the Seth Raynor Society, Geoff Shackelford, Jeff Jacobs, my fellow members at the St. Andrews Golf Club, my wonderful friends in France: Edwige, Gerard, Stella Mathis, and Theo; Bryan Caudle, Cornish, Mungeam and Gerrish; Jenna Beik, Nancy Powers, Dennis Parent, and all the good people at the Middletown Post Office, and, of course, Rebecca Graf.

Chris Gonsalves thanks his wife, Sung Cho, for being all of his inspiration; his dad, Albert Gonsalves, for keeping his golf game in check; and his savior, Jesus Christ, for, well, everything. Special thanks also go to David Humphrey, whose patience and guidance made me not only a better writer and a better golfer, but a better man as well. Also, thanks to Ken and Heidi Montigny, Mike and Christine Goulart, Mickey and Andree Goulart, Miles Goulart, Paul Berberian, Blanche Pepin, Kathi Gathercole, Monique Bradley, all the folks at the Kinsale Inn, Dennis Fisher, David and Ann Humphrey, Mike Zimmerman, Rob O'Regan, the Pasta House, David Sendler, Donna Scaglione, Max and Sam Burt, Scot Petersen, Mattapoisett Congregational Church, Lawrence Walsh, Chris Ruddy, Cable Neuhaus, Ken Williams, and the whole gang at Newsmax, Carmen Nobel, Ian Anderson, Martin Guitars, the City of Palm Beach Gardens, Pa Raffa, PGA National, Richie and everyone at Turk's Seafood, North Lake Presbyterian Church, Christ Fellowship, the Thirsty Turtle and the Brass Ring, the 2004 Boston Red Sox, and, of course, Bootsy and Muffin.

The authors also wish to acknowledge that Jeff Burt had not a single thing to do with the researching, writing, and editing of this book, no matter what he tells his friends and family.

About the Authors

Anthony Pioppi is a contributing editor for Golfdom and editor-at-large for Golfdom Europe.

From 1985 to 1998, Pioppi was a general-assignment news reporter, sportswriter, and police reporter for newspapers in Massachusetts, New Hampshire, and Connecticut. In 1998 he left writing to work on golf course grounds crews in Florida and Connecticut. Pioppi returned to writing in 2000 and since then has contributed to a number of golf magazines in the United States and the United Kingdom, writing about such topics as golf course architecture and maintenance, as well as golf travel.

Pioppi is also the author of *To the Nines,* a celebration of notable and memorable nine-hole golf courses throughout the United States. It was nominated for the U.S. Golf Association's Herbert Warren Wind Book Award.

He is also a golf architecture consultant and executive director of the Seth Raynor Society.

Pioppi, his Fender Stratocaster guitar, and his vintage Ampeg amplifier live a less-than-quiet existence in Middletown, Connecticut.

Chris Gonsalves has spent two decades writing about murder, mayhem . . . and golf.

As a waterfront columnist and crime reporter for The *Standard-Times* in New Bedford, Massachusetts, Chris spent countless hours prowling the deliciously spooky cobblestone streets of the historic Whaling City, a favorite haunt of Herman Melville and a cadre of lesser known spirits of the sea.

Later he covered luxury lifestyles as executive editor of *Gulfshore Life Magazine* in Naples, Florida, a city with more golf holes per capita than any place in America.

He lives in and works from the PGA National resort community in Palm Beach Gardens, Florida, where he's been known, late at night, to summon the undead on the championship course with his Martin acoustic and some tawny port. He always finds the famous Bear Trap holes a spine-chilling experience . . . day or night.

CBS golf analyst and Senior PGA Tour player **Peter Oosterhuis** got his start in broadcasting with Sky Sports in Great Britain, analyzing PGA Tour events from a London studio. He also worked for the venerable BBC at the 1996 and 1997 Open Championships. For three years beginning in 1995, Oosterhuis was the lead analyst for the Golf Channel coverage of the PGA European Tour, reporting from some ninety events.

Prior to his telecasting career, Oosterhuis was one of the leading players in Great Britain and Europe. He was a member of six Ryder Cup teams—1971, '73, '75, '77, and '81—and was unbeaten in his first seven singles matches. Oosterhuis stood atop the PGA European Tour Order of Merit for four consecutive seasons, 1971 to 1974, a record that stood until 1997. He captured nineteen international tournaments and was the runner-up in the 1974 and 1982 Open Championships.

Between providing commentary, participating in tournaments, and taking part in corporate events, Oosterhuis enjoys traveling with his wife, Ruth Ann.